Ca  Wilderness

Steve Bodansky

Also by Steve and Vera Bodansky

Extended Massive Orgasm: How to Give and Receive Sensual Pleasure

The Illustrated Guide to Extended Massive

Instant Orgasm: Excitement at First Touch

To Bed or Not to Bed

Extended Massive Life: A True Love Story and More

Extended Massive Orgasm: The Novel

Pigetry

Universe of Love: Poems of Yin and Yang

Switch Pitcher: Evolution of Darwin

Orgasm Matters

Love and Alzheimer's

Orbit: Looking for Libido

If You Then I: Rhymes with Love

Call of the Wilderness: copyright 2024

Chapter 1
Phoebe

Angels were singing in perfect harmony. It actually was some Gregorian chants playlist of music that she was listening to on her blue tooth speaker headphones, but with her eyes closed she imagined a choir of angels in an idyllic setting. She had decided only recently to be more laid back, not to fight the constant metaphoric windmills that seemed to churn up and create some havoc, both minor and major in what she used to call her life.

Phoebe had been reading in a number of spiritual books, and they all told her the same message in somewhat different words: "Let it be." "Let it go." "Lighten up." "Enjoy what is." "Be the witness."

She had even recently gone to one of those spiritual courses on a beach in Mexico. It seemed easier to let go and be, when you are with a bunch of likeminded folks that were all at similar crossroads in their journey. The trick was to take that feeling and understanding with her when she returned to her home in California.

Listening to the sweet music was one of the ways she used to put her back into that state of open awareness.

The phone rang. It was loud enough that she could make out the disturbance. For a brief moment she became annoyed at the interruption, then quickly changed her mind back to acceptance.

Before answering the phone she decided that whomever it was on the other end that she would use it as an opportunity to enjoy what is, and to create something good for whoever was calling. Maybe it was a call from the wilderness that she had dreamt of.

She saw from the caller ID that it was her friend Rachel's number highlighted, not exactly a call from the wilderness. Rachel was her oldest friend from her elementary school days, PS 179 in New York's public school system. They had even gone to high school together before Phoebe branched out, went to college at Columbia for pre-journalism, and met her husband.

After college Phoebe and her husband, also a journalist, did a lot of traveling as correspondents, both together and apart, and Phoebe was hardly in New York any more. She had left New York for good to go to California and be around her family after her husband was killed. Phoebe answered the phone.

"Hi Phoebes, can I talk to you for a minute?"

"Sure, I wasn't doing anything but listening to the angels singing on my Bluetooth. What gives?"

"What? Angels? Oh never mind," Rachel quickly got to the gist of her call. "I met this man on a dating site last week. He seems almost perfect, but I am worried that maybe he is not all what he claims to be. I am afraid to go meet him in person because if he is not this perfect person, then I will become hopeless. This way I can still have hope. Maybe it's best to wait. What do you think Phoebe?"

"Have you talked with him by phone, or *Zoom,* or anything? You can always regain hope. There is a large supply of it in the universe."

"That's funny, and we did have a phone conversation last night, and he wants to meet me in person, and take me out to dinner. He sounded sincere, but you can't really tell these days."

"Well, Rache, it seems to me that the next step is to either meet him in person, or to do a visual phone call, though I am not crazy about those visual connections. You don't have to go to dinner. You can meet for coffee or something less threatening. But I think being that you are in your mid thirties now, you are a grown woman, and can take the small risk to have a dinner with this guy. If you don't like him at least you can get a good meal out of it, plus somehow make his life better for having met you. If he is a complete liar and phony, you can always tell him that you have a migraine headache and split, pardon the pun."

"I knew that you were the right person to call Phoebes. I will accept his invitation then. How is your love life going, with that guy Jack, I think that was his name, you know the one that you met at that yoga retreat? The last time we spoke you were communicating with him, though he lives in Portland or Eugene, some place in Oregon."

"Thanks for asking. We are still friends, but neither one of us were that involved, and the long distance thing, even though not that long, was too long to keep the embers glowing, so I am available again for someone new and hopefully closer."

"You deserve someone wonderful after losing your husband like that," Rachel said.

"I don't believe in deserve, I believe in attraction and acceptance Rache, but thanks for the kind thought, I know what you mean. I will be attracting someone special for me soon. I can feel it. I got to go now...........Bye."

Phoebe felt that her meditation time must have been over, and decided to take a walk, perhaps get a cup of coffee in one of the nice coffee shops that keep springing up downtown. She gazed in the mirror before she left her nice home. Phoebe had gotten a huge death's benefit check from *ABC,* actually *Disney,* and had not spent it until recently, when she decided to buy a home of her own in San Cisco in Marin County near San Francisco. She liked what she saw in the mirror. Her face was radiant for some reason, though she wasn't wearing any makeup, and her dark hair was smooth and not acting up, as it did sometimes. Her clothes, which were a pair of tights and a form fitting top, looked good on her, showing her toned physique.

It wasn't real warm out, but it wasn't cold either, being a pleasant late winter Saturday in March in Northern California, sunny as usual. Phoebe put on a light jacket and a nice designer hat that her young supermodel friend in the home next to hers back in New York had given her as a present.

Phoebe walked the few blocks it took to get to the little downtown area of San Cisco in the middle of Marin County, with pep in her step. The streets were pretty empty of cars this early in the afternoon. The birds that were cacophonous in the early morning and early evening were basically quiet. The wind was quiet too and the sun warmed her gently, as she moved her body.

She decided to take a table outside the coffee shop, and watch the passersby. There was a cute elderly couple holding hands, dressed almost alike. Phoebe thought that they must have been together a long time. She had the negative thought that she wished Daniel and her could have grown old together like that. It was only for a split second, and she caught herself thinking that, and realized that to want anything other than the way it was, was foolish, and that new thought that she also was aware of, put a smile on her face.

There was a young woman on an electric scooter passing along on the sidewalk. Phoebe wondered how much exercise that actually was. She went inside the shop to order her drink.

There was a new young guy with a bad complexion taking the orders for coffee when she finally went inside. The usual cashier that Phoebe had built a rapport with, a young woman who reminded her of her friend Rachel, was actually preparing the drinks. Phoebe caught her eye and she nodded. Ellen, the name of the barista, said some code words to the cashier and Phoebe didn't have to add anything verbal, just pay for the drink and leave a tip in the tip jar.

Ellen handed Phoebe her hot mocha with chai, mentioning that she got a raise and was now the store manager. Phoebe congratulated her.

"Have a good one," Ellen said, as Phoebe turned to walk back outside to her table.

Phoebe really disliked that sentence. It seemed like everybody was using it these days, and it felt to her that when someone said that, it was on rote, kind of mindless, and not really felt. It was a way of dismissing someone instead of saying a friendly goodbye. The pimply cashier had just said it to her as well, and she hadn't said anything to him.

Phoebe debated with herself whether she should say something to Ellen. She decided that she kind of liked Ellen, and would tell her how she felt.

Phoebe turned back to face Ellen, "Thanks Ellen, I appreciate the good wishes. I prefer however, just a simple *goodbye,* or *see you later,* than *have a good one,* or *have a great day.* I don't know what it is about that phrase, but it feels unreal and dismissive, even though I'm sure you meant it in a friendly way. I never use it myself anymore, and thought because I like you that I'd tell you how I feel, if that is all right?"

Ellen smiled, "No, that is perfect. I've been saying it too often anyway, and think it is true what you say. I do kind of go blank after saying it. I appreciate your feedback; I like you too, and if I ever say it to you again please remind me again. I almost said *have a great day* again, but I will see you later."

Phoebe went back outside, sat down at her still empty table and slowly drank her hot beverage. She felt vindicated or at least a bit happier after Ellen responded the way she did. A tall, nice looking, lightly tanned man walked into the store and nodded at her as he went by. Phoebe nodded back.

He came out a few minutes later with his steaming paper cup of coffee. He slowly walked up to her table, and asked, "Do you mind if I share this table with you?"

Phoebe liking his vibes, and the closer he got, the cuter he appeared. She responded, "Be my guest. I'm Phoebe, and you are?"

"Thanks Phoebe, my name is Isaiah. What are you drinking?"

"That sounds biblical. I'm just drinking a mocha with chai, Isaiah," Phoebe flirted, as she gazed into his eyes briefly then back to her coffee.

"That practically matches my skin color," Isaiah flirted back, looking straight at Phoebe's face, and noticing how pretty she was. "By the way, that is a nice hat you have on. As far as how I was named, that is a biblical story."

Phoebe chuckled, liking that he noticed her exclusive, one of a kind hat. She had the thought that people still were too fixated on skin color and wondered if she should comment back or just move the conversation along, which is what she decided to do.

"How would you describe the taste of your drink?" Phoebe asked, remembering that men liked to answer how questions and women were good at what queries?

"That's funny you should ask, because I was jolted by that last swig," Isaiah responded. "It tastes better than usual, maybe because my senses are heightened from just meeting you. It tastes a bit creamy to my mouth, even though I did not add any cream. It has a trace of bitterness, but tastes sweeter than usual with a hint of acidity. The aroma is kind of chocolaty and fruity at the same time, similar to cherries I think, with a hint of lavender. It is hot and awakens my mouth that even spreads to my skin after swallowing. It reminds me of a perfect spring day with furry creatures awakening and running through the forest. What are you getting from your mocha?"

"I'm impressed; that is a mouthful," Phoebe laughed. "I feel warm all over, like your fuzzy creatures sunbathing. It tastes bittersweet in a good way. I love dark chocolate, practically with no sugar. I'm going to change the subject now, if that is all right with you?"

"Sure," Isaiah answered, "and I said furry not fuzzy, but they are almost the same. Which subject?"

"How about what you like to do, and what kind of work are you into?" Phoebe asked.

"I like being outdoors, in the forest with those fuzzy furry feathery creatures. I actually have a job with the *California Fish and Wildlife Department,* working on land management and how to best reintroduce and maintain gray wolves into the wilderness areas of Northern California. My mom lives here in town, and I'm visiting her for the weekend. It's her birthday today. This small town is as close to civilization that I usually get. How about you?"

Before Phoebe could answer his question, an attractive woman with a brown Labrador Retriever on leash was walking by. The pooch was pulling on the leash in order to go over to Isaiah. He patted it on the head and scratched behind its ears. The dog was almost purring like a cat.

"Her name is Classie. I've never heard her make those sounds before. You must be a real dog whisperer," the woman stated.

"Maybe, I never thought of it in those terms, but dogs do seem to like me," Isaiah responded, noticing that Phoebe was getting a bit antsy over the interruption.

Wow, Phoebe thought to herself. I think I am having a *good one*, or a *great day*. The call of the wilderness is calling me, as I predicted.

Phoebe liked this new guy, but she wasn't sure how much she should reveal of herself. She had been a journalist and had lived in New York, and traveled all over the world with her husband, who was also a famous journalist, who was tragically killed in an explosion about three years earlier in Afghanistan. She had relocated permanently to Marin, California, living part time with her mom and step-dad, and at times with her dad and step mom, before recently moving out again, and living in her own place. She decided to tell Isaiah the truth once the woman pulled the reluctant Classie from Isaiah.

"I'm not working full time at the moment. I used to be a journalist for *ABC* news. This is Phoebe Granger, reporting from Tel Aviv. You may have seen me on TV. My husband Daniel was killed by a drone strike after he was taken hostage by the Taliban in Afghanistan a number of years ago."

"I'm sorry to hear about that," Isaiah said, remembering the story about the famous news reporter Daniel Granger and his beautiful news reporter wife. They were both top notch reporters and she quit after her husband died so dreadfully. "I remember that story. It wasn't that long ago. The Taliban had him as a hostage and we bombed one of the Taliban leaders at a farmhouse, and they happened to be holding your husband as hostage in that same place. So you are Phoebe Granger. I remember seeing both you and your husband on TV at my mom's home. You looked different, still very beautiful, but with a lot more makeup on than you are wearing now. I'm not a big fan of makeup, but I had a crush on you anyhow. Gee, this is funny telling you that to your face," Isaiah said, blushingly.

"I'm flattered that you thought I was beautiful. It seems longer than a few years, a lifetime ago to me. I've done a few freelance stories for online and print magazines, but nothing steady. I once did a story about the wolves in Montana too." Phoebe had the thought that maybe she could do a story on Isaiah and his work, but she did not bring that up yet.

"Really, that's wonderful, I mean that you are familiar with wolves, not that your husband died of course. I am again so sorry for you," Isaiah responded awkwardly, feeling that he just put his foot in his mouth. "I actually studied wolf maintenance in Montana as well, from a guy named Hootman who had studied with Adolph Murie in the *Denali National Park* in Alaska, although it was called *Mt. McKinley National Park* back then. Murie is known as the father of wolf tolerance and acceptance, and wrote numerous books on the protection of wolves and bears. He even helped create the *Grand Teton National Park* in Montana."

"Yes, I've heard of Murie, but did not read any of his books. I only spent a few days on research for the article, but it was also with Hootman in Montana. Small world isn't it," Phoebe recounted, glad that the topic had changed from her tragic past to something more fun.

"Wow, that is amazing." Isaiah responded, and then asked. "Do you know how Hootman got his name."

"I don't," Phoebe answered, but I bet that you are going to tell me."

Chapter 2
Hootman

"**Bill** Hootman's real name wasn't really Hootman either. He was christened William Oliver, but when he was in his teens, his Scottish friend Ben McDonald had nicknamed him Hootman because Billy was often under the hood of the different cars that his dad Benjamin fixed in the repair garage adjacent to their house. Billy or Hootman was becoming an excellent mechanic himself, but his girlfriend at the time of his junior year in high school did not want him being covered in grime and grease all the time."

"Hootman then decided to become an English major. That didn't last long either. He had been fascinated with wolves and their negative associations in fairy tales since he was a little kid when his mom would read to him at night to help him fall asleep. He was drawn to the story about *Little Red Riding Hood* and would talk about it to whoever would listen; hence another reason for his nickname. He felt sorry for Riding Hood at first, but later also thought that she was responsible for her comeuppance. After all, Hootman would relate, she went blabbing to the wolf about where her grandmother lived. Who talks to wolves anyhow, especially in the forest when alone? No one was too interested in Hootman's ramblings, except maybe his friend Ben, but that did not deter him from talking about it either."

Isaiah continued with his story. "Later when he thought about it, it was just another example of putting a wolf in the role of a criminal; so killing them could be justified. That's when he decided to go into biology in his second year in college, and help restore wolves to their natural habitats. Hootman learned all he could abut wolves. He understood that the Gray Wolf had made the same trek that some Asian people had made to America; only it wasn't really America yet. They traveled over the same land bridge that connected the two continents. Only they had done it many thousands, perhaps hundreds of thousand of years earlier. The wolf had little competition, that is, before humans came to share their territories. There were saber tooth tigers, grizzly bears, even dire wolves that enjoyed the same prey as them, but because wolves hunted and traveled in packs, they were pretty much left alone. For some reason the dire wolves became extinct. They were slightly larger with even a stronger jaw than their cousins, but were bested and outlasted by their relatives."

"Furthermore," Isaiah continued, "there were plenty of game available, including the large ungulates or hooved animals, such as: elk, bison, moose, reindeer, and musk oxen. There were also smaller ungulates such as: white tailed deer, pronghorn antelopes, sheep, roe and mule deer. Beavers, rabbits, rodents, other small mammals and even birds are sometimes fed upon, though the wolves prefer the larger prey, especially the elk.

Hootie or Hootman went to the University of Montana and received his degree in biology. He did his doctorate there as well, focusing of course on wolves and their management. He spent a couple of years in Alaska, learning from Adolph Murie. This was about the time that wolves had been put on the federal most endangered list in 1973. There had been a preliminary law introduced in the 1960s, helping whatever remained of the wolf population to be protected, thanks to Murie.

Before that, wolves were considered a menace. There were over 2 million wolves in the lower 48 states in the early nineteenth century. As more settlers moved west, the territories enjoyed by wolves became less and less. Now territory inhabited by wolves is approximately 10% of what it once was, if that much. The federal government placed bounties on wolves in the late 1800s, and by the first quarter of the twentieth century wolf populations over the United States had been almost completely eradicated. Luckily, Canada still retained some of its wolf population, about 50,000 of them, although they are still hunted when they leave the national and the provincial parks. Their numbers are also drastically reduced from what it once was. Most of the wolves that inhabit the Northern Rockies migrated, or were deliberately brought in from Canada," Isaiah finally finished with his story, after occasionally taking a sip of coffee to wet his mouth and throat.

Chapter 3
Isaiah

"Can I apologize for hogging the conversation? I am usually quite quiet. I guess once I get started talking about wolves, I really lose track of everything else for a while. I hope that I did not bore you." Isaiah asked.

"You can apologize if you like, but no, on the contrary, I enjoyed learning more about Hootman, and about wolves in general. My husband was a kind of a lone wolf until I met him, though he was a bit of a womanizer, and so I feel very close to wolves, and also want to help them. I've always loved big dogs, starting with my dad's love for dogs. My first dog that I had on my own, my senior year in college was a large Husky mix, a shelter dog that I called Wolfie," Phoebe shared.

"That's great, thanks for being receptive to my story, and I will withdraw my apology then," Isaiah responded, and then asked. "Is your dad alive? You mentioned that you stayed with your mom and step dad."

"Yes, he lives fairly close by, also in Marin County. I am actually closer with him than my mom, who can be a bitter pill at times, but I love them both. I stayed with him and his wife for a while too. My parents divorced when I was a senior in high school. They both came out to California from New York after I got married. I followed them here after Daniel died. My dad started his own brewing company after they divorced. He is doing quite well financially now, though he had a hard time making enough money to keep my mom happy when they were together. The break-up was good for the both of them. My mom married a rich older guy and my dad has a wife, his age that also is into brewing. I never liked beer very much, but theirs is better than any others that I have tasted. It's really been nice getting to know you. The next time you are in town, give me a call," Phoebe anted up to see if Isaiah wanted to see her again.

Isaiah called her bet and raised it, "I will still be around a couple more days. How about tomorrow night for dinner, or even better, a walk on the beach, the time of day of your choosing, and then some food. My mom's birthday party is tonight, but I'm totally free tomorrow. I really would love to see you again before leaving."

"Wow, you are persuasive, and I am persuaded," Phoebe responded, noticing her effect on Isaiah. "How about an early morning walk, like around 8AM, leave around 7AM, and then brunch. I'll text you my address and you can pick me up and we can go to *Stinson Beach* first, if that is all right with you?"

"Yes, I get up early anyhow and that would be great. The birthday party tonight is a dinner party so I'll be able to get plenty of sleep. I'd invite you to the party, but I don't think you'd have a great time there. I know this cool beach by Bolinas that is hard to find if you don't know the way, if you'd like to check that out? I also know a great place in Olema to have brunch," Isaiah responded.

"That is a great idea. I've got plans tonight anyhow, and yes, I've always wanted to go to Bolinas, but they have no signs there, so I've always stayed away, except for once when I got lost," Phoebe said.

Isaiah felt like kissing and hugging this beautiful person he just met, but thought that she might think he was being too forward, and just said a friendly good bye, no mention of having a great day, thank goodness, after getting Phoebe's phone information. They walked away in opposite directions, each one feeling a huge buzz of excitement and love. Cupid or whatever had pierced them both.

Isaiah had never felt this way before. He felt like a dose of adrenaline had been administered without his knowledge. It was a good feeling, and he could feel the tingling sensation all over his skin and beneath. He thought he might go for a run. He drove a short distance to a hilly area that he liked to run in and did just that.

Everything about the run felt exhilarating. The green colors of the trees and grass and early spring flowers were reflecting amazing colors back to his retina. His lung capacity was more voluminous than usual and he did not feel tired. He could spot birds high up in the canopy in nests feeding their young. The birds were chattering almost continuously. It felt like their songs and sounds were personally communicating and congratulating him for his enjoyment. He thought to himself that he just might be in love for the first time in his life.

Chapter 4
Phoebe

Dare I feel so good? Phoebe thought to herself, as she also felt amazing. She hadn't felt this way since she had met Daniel many years earlier, and not even close to this good since he had passed. She walked home with even more of a bounce in her step than when she had gone out. Phoebe called her friend Rachel after getting situated at home. Waiting for Rachel to pick up the phone, she noticed that the paintings on the wall seemed more colorful than she could remember. She had a couple prints from Marc Chagall and a few originals from local artists. They all appeared so vivid and seemed to be more alive than ever before.

Rachel finally answered, "So what did I do to deserve two phone calls with you on the same day?"

"I just met him. Remember I just told you that I had a hunch that I was going to meet someone soon. I didn't realize it would be this soon. He just appeared at the coffee shop while I was sitting at one of those tables out front of the café. I noticed him going into the café. He was tall, strong looking, with a gentle but robust intensity to him."

"Kind of like a strong, but mellow cup of coffee," Rachel kidded.

"That is funny. His skin color is like a light mocha and he also remarked about looking like that color. I don't like to put much attention on skin color, or coffee resemblance, but the association makes it difficult not to," Phoebe confided.

"So what is he like besides the coffee reference, and what are you going to do with him? Is he local? Can you give me his name? I can look up his credentials for you," Rachel bombarded her friend with questions.

"I just met him. I don't even know his last name yet. We did make a date for tomorrow, a walk on the beach, and then brunch. He is an early riser, as I am. He does not live in town, but he is visiting his mom, who does. It's her birthday today. One part of my checklist is that the next man in my life should have a good relationship with his mother, the same way that Daniel did, if she happens to still be alive, but not too close to her. He lives up north in the wilderness, and works for the *California Fish and Wildlife Department*. He is into wolf protection. Remember that article that I did about the wolves in Montana for *National Geographic*? Well, he studied with those same people and we share that," Phoebe responded.

"So are you planning to live in the wilderness with Grizzly Adams?" Rachel kidded her friend.

"As I said, I just met Isaiah. I'll take it step by step, and see how it goes. I did have more than one thought already about how it would be in the forest with him, so yeah it is a possibility I suppose."

"So he does have a name, Isaiah, just not a last name yet. I am really so happy for you Phoebes. I think I read somewhere that Isaiah was the only prophet to show up in the new and old testaments. I know that you don't like the word deserve, but you do deserve someone exceptional in my rating system. I hope your walk goes well tomorrow. I made a date with Connor for next week, so I will keep you informed on that. I want to speak to you tomorrow after your date, to see how Grizzly, I'm kidding, I mean Isaiah did."

They said their good byes and ended the conversation. Phoebe chuckled at the Grizzly Adams comment, though she thought that Isaiah would look great in a suit or any kind of uniform or naked for that matter, and she fantasized about that.

Chapter 5
Isaiah

Everything was sill extra bright and wonderful. Isaiah got back in his Ford pick up. He had just gotten a new hybrid model and was glad that he wasn't burning up so much fossil fuel anymore. He drove back to his mom's place, still feeling elated and high. His mom was a very kind woman. She had raised Isaiah to be a compassionate young man with a lot of help from her parents and her sister. His mother's name was Kenisha. She had Isaiah when she was only 17 and Isaiah never did meet his dad, who hightailed it out of there when he found out that Kenisha was pregnant. He had said that he would always use condoms, but the one time that they didn't was enough. Kenisha believed women should have the ability to choose whether to have an abortion or not, but she chose not to, and was glad of her decision, though it did make her life way more complicated.

    Kenisha graduated high school that same year and went into the *University of San Francisco* nursing program on a full scholarship. She was a good student and graduated in 4 years at the age of 21. She came home from school to their home in San Rafael, often after a long day there, and spent quality time with her son, when she did not have to study. Isaiah was also close to his grandparents Rose and old Ben, and Kenisha's sister Katrina, who watched over him when Kenisha was at school. Ben had played a few years in the NFL, but retired early after sustaining a torn ACL. He then taught PE at the local San Rafael high school and was an assistant on the football team there before becoming the head coach. He was actually the head coach there when Isaiah matriculated.

Isaiah was also gifted in football and made the starting team in his freshman year at the school. He was a two way player and played at wide receiver on offense and a linebacker for the defense. Ben was very proud of his grandson and saw him as the MVP of the team.

Isaiah was recruited by a number of colleges, but decided not to go into football, as Ben died from a brain aneurism at the end of Isaiah's senior year. Isaiah was devastated, as well as his mother and grandmother, who always believed that Ben was the strongest, kindest, and gentlest person that they knew. Isaiah believed that playing football, especially in the pros was what killed Ben, and he didn't want to follow that lifestyle, even though it made him popular. Isaiah also had good grades and got a full academic scholarship to go to *Humboldt State*, part of the California State University system in coastal Northern California, though he did turn down *Stanford's* football scholarship offer after first having accepted it.

Isaiah was an excellent student and majored in Environmental Sciences as an undergraduate. He felt a genuine call of the wild and wanted to do something for the mammals, even the birds and fish that were under pressure from human civilization encroaching on the wilderness.

Isaiah graduated with honors and was accepted at the *University of Montana's* Ecology and Evolution doctoral program in Missoula. He continued his studies on large mammals as well as taking all the required science courses. He knew what he wanted to do. The second semester of his first year there he took a course from Hootman, or William Oliver, as he was officially known. Isaiah really respected Hootman and the work that he had been doing with wolves, and selected Hootman to be his supervisor/mentor/advisor. Hootman eagerly accepted Isaiah as his student/protégé.

Isaiah worked the next three years under Hootman's tutelage. They were out in the field together for a good part of the time, and Isaiah was smart enough to learn everything that he could from Hootman, and from the wolves that he was introduced to. The wolves were collared and they were able to track them at all times, though this was not necessarily as easy as it sounded, as wolves have a large area that they roam in.

The wolves seemed to like Hootman just as he loved them, and had allowed him access to their den when pups were being born. He and his small group were able to collar the pups with a tracking device once they were old enough, which was when they had grown substantially, but were still less than a year old. It was time for a new litter to be born when Isaiah went into the field with Hootman that first spring. They found the pack that Hootman had been following, and the wolves allowed Hootman to bring his new friend into the den to see the pups. Normal gestation for a wolf, similar to a dog, is only a little over 2 months.

The pack of wolves outside of the den came up to Hootman and his new friend and smelled them, and determined that they were friends, one old and one new. The alpha male that Hootman called Rocky even licked Hootman's hand, allowing them to pass into the den, appearing to Isaiah as a proud papa. The wolves let them crawl into the den and say hello to mom, whom Hootman named Zelda, who was feeding her pups. Two of the pups were suckling and the other two seemed to be sleeping. They were smaller than Isaiah had thought they would be, probably weighing less than a pound each. Their eyes were still closed over, and did not respond to the miner's light on top of Hootman's hat. The mom recognized Hootman as her friend, and also licked his hand, and did the same to Isaiah. Isaiah found this relationship with the wild fascinating, and really enjoyed being away from civilization. Isaiah was in love with wolves more than ever.

Besides working at the University and tracking wolves, Hootman had set up a non-profit group that he called *Friends of the Wolf*. Hootman's wife Lacy was actually a lawyer and had done the work to legally set up this group. It included a veterinarian who donated his services, and an ex special ops sharpshooter that assisted in sedating the animals. They even had a local business magnate who owned a helicopter, if they had to travel quickly. They had a couple volunteer lobbyists to petition the government of Montana and of the Federal government on retainer, plus a couple other volunteers to do paper work, and occasionally help out in the field. The *Friends* would sometimes have to talk to ranchers, so that they did not retaliate against the wolves. They raised money to pay off any ranchers that did lose any of their animals to wolf pack raids, which was actually infrequent and less than one would expect.

In Isaiah's second year in Missoula, Hootman invited him to live with his family in the outskirts of that city. The Olivers are a family of four, but by the time Isaiah showed up, Hootman and Lacy's children were already out of the nest. They let Isaiah stay in their son Sean's old room. Isaiah stayed there while he attended classes, and used it as his home base, as he would spend much of his time out in the field. For the first year and a half he would go out with Hootman regularly to attend to Rocky and Zelda's pack, plus a couple other packs that Hootman followed. The last year in Montana, Hootman let Isaiah out on his own much of the time.

Isaiah wrote his thesis on determining specific DNA markers of preyed upon animals that turned up in wolf scat. Much of the work had already been done previously, but was less than foolproof. Working in collaboration with a couple post docs in the genetics lab, they found a way to find easier markers from mitochondrial DNA that were more specific, and created a quicker test result. Hootman had previously trained a German Shepard to help find the scats, which are not that obvious to humans doing the tracking. The friendly Shepard was named Rex, and when out hunting scat, Isaiah would use the pooch to sniff out the wolf scat. He collected the scat fairly quickly this way, and was able to finish his thesis before the four years of his doctoral program. His thesis was well accepted and he obtained his degree.

Isaiah moved back to California to implement the knowledge that he obtained working under Hootman. He got a job almost immediately in Northern California, getting employed with the *California Fish and Wildlife Department.* He already had been working there for around 7 years when he meets Phoebe.

He spent much of the time out in the field, often in solitary pursuits. He had numerous girlfriends throughout his college education, but never felt the emotions that he was feeling after meeting Phoebe for just those few minutes. It made him wonder for the first time what it would be like to have a partner in life. He knew that wolf packs had an alpha male and an alpha female that led the pack together. They were usually the only wolves of the pack that mated and had offspring. He also had been thinking for the first time in his life about having offspring of his own. He knew that he was jumping the gun, but he understood that he really wasn't fully in charge of which thoughts arrived in his consciousness.

Kenisha was back from the beauty salon when Isaiah got home. She noticed a sparkle in Isaiah's eyes that she hardly recognized. "Did you see some wolf cubs when you went out this morning? There are some positive vibrations emanating from you that I hardly recognize, and I don't know what else would make you so happy. Oh I got it. You met some woman today, and she put a spell on you," Kenisha added perceptively.

"I got to hand it to you Mom, you truly are observant. I went to the coffee shop downtown, and there was this beautiful radiant woman sitting there alone. I walked up to her, asked if I could sit down, which I never do, and she was more than receptive. We talked for over an hour and I have a date to meet her for a walk on the beach tomorrow. I can't believe that you picked that up and could see that in me so quickly. I'm not going to play poker with you," Isaiah exclaimed.

"Oh Honey, I know how dedicated you are to your work, but to find a soul mate in this world will make a difference in the quality of your life. I am even still hopeful that I will meet someone one of these days. You have been a joy to me ever since you were born, and nothing could make me happier than to see you as happy as you are now. You just gave me a wonderful birthday present," Kenisha acknowledged.

"We don't know what will be the eventual outcome of my meeting Phoebe. I don't want to get my hopes up too high, and then have them crash, but I have never felt this way after meeting someone, as I do now. She is smart, attentive, and beautiful, as I said. She is a widower, no children, and seems genuine, if I can judge correctly. You remember that reporter Daniel Granger who died in Afghanistan a few years ago? Phoebe was his wife, also a reporter, and I used to watch her on *ABC News* too," Isaiah responded. "But today is your birthday, and I want to put some attention on you. I didn't want to invite Phoebe to your dinner party tonight, though I did have that thought. I also thought it would be better to see her one on one tomorrow, and that she would be more comfortable doing that than meeting your friends and relatives so soon. If all goes well, I do want you to meet her as soon as can be arranged."

"Of course I remember the Grangers. She is very beautiful and talented. That was so tragic. I think you made a wise decision there, although I would like to meet her too. If she turns out as perfect as the way it seems now, we will have plenty of time for that," Kenisha added.

Chapter 6
Phoebe

Frozen, yet fluid, that's how it seemed. Time seemed to stand still for the next few hours. Phoebe was eager to see Isaiah again. She was usually patient, but this new event had triggered her body into hyper drive. Thoughts were careening around her mind like a torrential rainstorm.

Her past life flashed in front of her in bits and pieces, especially her life with Daniel. Her husband Daniel had first told her that he had been an orphan, and that his parents had died in a jet crash returning from Jerusalem about two years before she had enrolled at the University. This was totally fabricated by Daniel. His parents were alive and well, and still living in a mansion in Scarsdale. His dad was a lawyer and Daniel was a little embarrassed about his right wing politics, therefore he often pretended to be an orphan. Phoebe almost left him after she found out that he had lied to her, but forgave him when he came clean and begged her for forgiveness.

Daniel was her TA at *Columbia* her first year there, getting his doctorate in Journalism and International Affairs, while she was attaining her Bachelor's degree. She had a similar response in her body when they had first met, which she had now felt again when meeting Isaiah. She wasn't the only girl in her class who was infatuated with their brilliant political science teacher. He was technically a grad student, but was held in high esteem by the University, and given extra responsibilities. When their eyes locked as she approached him after class to ask him a question, it was as if instant glue was applied to them. Phoebe had to wait to start officially dating her teacher the semester after being in his class, in order to follow University protocol. They still met for lunch and other unofficial business under the guise of classwork.

After about only a month of officially dating she moved into Daniel's apartment that he shared with another graduate student. Phoebe enrolled in the 2 year Master's program at *Columbia's* journalism school, after graduating with her Bachelor's degree. She now wondered, as her past flashed before her, why it was called a bachelor's degree anyhow, probably another sexist viewpoint from the past. She chose part time rather than the quicker full time program, so that she could earn some money and get some valuable experience.

Daniel had gotten a high profile job working for *ABC News* in their New York City headquarters, and was being paid a healthy salary, so Phoebe was not necessarily in need of the extra cash, but she decided to stay in the longer program for the added skills provided by the working experience. Daniel was able to get Phoebe a part time job as his assistant, while she was still taking 2 classes a semester. They worked well together, and although his name would get top billing, he was always generously promoting Phoebe. They got married about a year after first meeting, in a small ceremony. Only her parents, and his parents, whom she finally met, plus a few friends of theirs, such as Rachel, attended.

After Phoebe graduated the *Columbia* journalist master's program, *ABC World News* hired her as a full time investigative reporter. Again degrees' named after male stereotypes, but she guessed a woman could be a master as well, even though when these titles were first used, only men went to universities. *ABC* had a number of talented and also very pretty young women working on their *World News* shows. Daniel had become one of the most relied upon members of the news team, and was often sent abroad to cover numerous world crises. They were no longer working together all the time, but when Daniel was not overseas, they still spent quite a bit of time together in the news room and at home.

Phoebe wondered why her life was flashing in front of her like this. She thought it must be the emotion of meeting Isaiah that had triggered these recollections, both fun, and some of anger of her past life with Daniel. She decided to do some yoga and do some more meditation that she had been doing earlier this morning before being interrupted. It took a while, but she became more grounded, and the careening thoughts slowed down to a mere trickle.

After eating a light supper, Phoebe read the beginning of the *Jungle Book* by Rudyard Kipling. Her dad had read it to her years before, when she was still a little girl. She really didn't remember much, and read the part about Mowgli being brought up by wolves, which is what she was really interested in, something to bring up with Isaiah the next day perhaps. Mowgli's wolf mother was named Raksha and his father wolf was called just that. Phoebe fell asleep and slept well, dreaming of welcoming wolves, and friendly dogs.

Chapter 7
Isaiah and Phoebe

Good morning, Isaiah felt he finally understood those words. Isaiah picked up Phoebe at exactly 7AM. The sun had not quite risen but the sky was already getting lighter, indicative of a new day dawning. Phoebe came out to join him and jumped in the car before Isaiah had a chance to get out of his seat and come around to open the door for her, which is what he had planned to do.

Isaiah felt like kissing and hugging her right then and there, as the chemistry was so strong, but did not want to come off as a too aggressive male. Phoebe could feel the energy intensely palpitating and coursing throughout her entire body, but did not want to come across as too needy or too wanton either, so she played it cool, as difficult as that was, at least at first.

She started the conversation by stating the usual social greetings and salutations, asking him how he was doing, etc.

Isaiah responded, "I've been thinking of you ever since we parted yesterday. I am not sure what happened, but you put a powerful spell over me Phoebe. Just now when I saw you again, coming toward the car, I wanted to jump out of the car and greet you with passion, but did not want to blow it with you. I felt like grabbing you and devouring you with my affection. However, I decided that the way you quickly got into the car that I should be more controlled. I have been around wolves for a long time now and they greet each other rather affectionately when they feel the desire, but we are humans and not wolves; so we do have that ability to be restrained when required."

Phoebe leaned in toward Isaiah. He could smell her magnificent body scent and fragrance. "I have been in a similar emotional state as you. I think that you put that spell on me, or perhaps it was Cupid. I did not want to ruin anything by going too fast either, but after you just told me your desires, I can admit mine too, and think we both can use a welcoming kiss for our thirsting lips."

At those last words they both leaned in some more and put their respective hands behind each other's heads and necks to stabilize the excitement. Isaiah breathed in deeply to take in full that magnificent scent of this beautiful being that was now embracing him. Phoebe let Isaiah make the first engagement with his lips, though from the viewpoint of a non existent third party, it would have been hard to tell who was the aggressor.

His gentle lips against hers sent an immediate armada of sensation all over her body from the top of her head to the tip of her toes and especially to her genitals, which were now wet and open. This seemed to last forever, though it was probably only for a few seconds. Phoebe retaliated by using her tongue to defend her mouth, and gently probe his lips with a circular reconnaissance, before probing only a short distance past his lines of defense.

Isaiah could feel the connection to his penis, which was very engorged, as she probed his mouth with her tongue. He received it as the gift that it was, accepting and embracing it with his own tongue, which now responded to her examination in some form of sexual dance inside of his mouth that he had never done or felt before.

After this outrageous osculation they both sat back in their seats and Isaiah started driving his truck west toward Highway 1 and the beaches. Neither of them spoke for a few minutes afterwards, staying in a zone of bliss, feeling the buzz upon their lips still reverberating in their bodies.

Finally Phoebe said, "I am not sure that we really have to say anything to verify what just happened, but that was so special and extraordinary that if we just go on like nothing happened we may lose a chance to immortalize our feelings."

"Wow, I still feel like we are kissing now. My lips are still all a buzz and your essence has deeply penetrated my being," Isaiah responded. Continuing, "I have never felt this way my entire life. I don't know how to process it fully, but there is something so strong going on both physically and spiritually that I was afraid to talk, thinking that it might disappear, but it only has gotten stronger since I have put it into words. Your lips are so tender, smooth, and luscious, and beckon me to them unswervingly. Your aromatic fragrant physicality pulls me to you with little regard for anything else."

"For being such a new sensation for you, which is hard to believe, you do have a way with words that ignites my very own soul into a vortex of ecstasy," Phoebe re responded enthusiastically. "My body is a buzz as well, and I too wish to embrace you with my whole being. We hardly know each other, but it feels like we always have and always will. I can't believe my own words but I am speaking metaphorically from my heart and not my brain, and do hope to learn all about you that I can. I had the thought that we could go to a motel to further explore each other's bodies, but think it best, again coming from my heart, to continue to the beach and walk and talk and perhaps kiss some more, and save the rest of the further exploration for later."

"I will do whatever you want, and what you want sounds great to me. I love being outside and being in a stuffy indoor motel room, although enticing, will not be as promising as sharing the sky and the ocean, and the redwoods that are in our immediate future. The indoor bliss can wait for another time," Isaiah agreed, as he drove onwards.

Isaiah slowly drove over *Mt. Tamalpais,* and the scenery was magnificent. "This mountain was named from the *Miwok* Native American tribe that lived here, and means bay or coast mountain in their language," Isaiah said.

"I did not know that. I always thought there must have been a person with that name, which seems funny now that you told me. Thanks for the education," Phoebe responded

It was always a nice scenic drive, but was even more so with this electric woman by his side. Phoebe felt comfortable enough to talk about her past, and also to be silent for a few minutes at a time in order to take in the beauty of the forest. She was a couple years older than Isaiah, and was the first time that she had been with a younger man.

Isaiah had googled her name after their meeting at the cafe, fondly remembering the beautiful reporter that he had seen on the TV news dozens of times, even though she wasn't wearing that makeup when they met yesterday. He remembered that he had thought that she was beautiful on the screen, and had a boyhood crush on her. He found Phoebe even more beautiful in person. He had found out a bit about her life story from the *Wikipedia* page, so was not surprised about some of the tragedy that she had gone through, when she related her story to him.

Phoebe told him how she was reading about Mowgli in Kipling's *The Jungle Book* and the bond that he had with the wolves.

Isaiah said, "Yes! I loved that story when I was a kid. It gave me fantasies and dreams of being taken in by a wolf pack, and living an adventurous life in the wilderness. I guess it was influential in my choice of vocations. I also went to a lecture in my teens that the environmentalist Farley Mowat gave. He is also one of my heroes. He wrote the book *Never Cry Wolf* about arctic wolves in Northern Canada. Although it is partly made-up, I like that he says that he never lets the facts get in the way of the truth. He is quite funny and his story really helped save wolves from becoming extinct in the mid twentieth century."

"I will have to check that out," Phoebe said. "Do you ever get lonely when you are out alone without contact with anyone for days?" she asked.

"Nope, I don't. I feel that I am surrounded by nature. I believe the trees and the sky and all the animals that I come across almost every minute are more than enough to grab my attention. I have never felt real close to another person, except for my mom, who I do speak to regularly, and also my grandparents and aunt who helped raise me. I have to admit, I felt lonely a bit after we parted yesterday, even though I was on some kind of a chemical high. You are sure powerful and a direct vehicle for what I call the source. I know it is so early in our relationship, if this even is a relationship, I guess it is, because what else would I call it, but you have put a loving magical spell on me that makes life seem even better than it was. I have never been so honest and straight with my feelings toward anyone before, so don't think I am just another Casanova trying to sweet talk you."

"That's funny," Phoebe said. "I don't think anyone would compare you to a Casanova or a Don Juan. As a matter of fact, I have decided that we are in a relationship. If anyone in this relationship were the seducer here, it would be me."

They remained quiet for the next few minutes. Isaiah could feel Phoebe in his loins and elsewhere. He was both excited yet more at peace than he had ever felt. Phoebe confessed that she had not had real meaningful sex since her husband passed away, and that she was fantasizing just then about having some with him.

"I can see that you were picking up on my thoughts, Isaiah," Phoebe assured him that what he felt was real. "You are very sensitive for someone who has never been in a significant relationship, and is one of the characteristics that drew me to you, both the bond-virginity and the sensitivity."

"I am amazed how much power you hold over me and how much I enjoy that. I've always felt that I had to be responsible for everything I did. It feels authentic to allow you the honor of steering me, and taking control of my engine," Isaiah said, with a sincere smile on his face.

They could see the ocean from the top of the cliff, and Isaiah stopped the car at a vista point overlook that could only fit the one vehicle. They got out of the car and the sky was a magnificent red orange toward the East, as the sun was just rising. They approached one another and executed a perfect full body hug. Isaiah could feel the electric vibrations emanating from Phoebe, especially from her pelvic region that was planted against the firmness of his, which she definitely felt. They stood entwined together like that for a who knows how many minutes, just breathing in the fresh ocean air, and feeling each other's bodies. They finally separated, and the sun had already risen way past the horizon.

Isaiah spoke first. "I have now had the best hug of my entire life to go along with the best kiss. You really are something else Phoebe."

"I too am amazed that we fit so perfectly together Isaiah. Your genuine response to my flirtations and intimacies are totally gratifying. It feels like my whole life has been in preparation for this exact moment. I've never felt so in tune with this dance that we call life."

They got back in the pickup, feeling more grounded, and drove down to the ocean road past *Stinson Beach*, where Isaiah made a left turn on some unnamed road, and a few minutes later they were parked at *Bolinas Beach*. The tide was getting lower so they could walk the entirety of the beach.

They each had a little back pack for their water bottles and warm skull caps that they immediately put on, as the temperature was a bit chilly this early in the morning. There was hardly anyone on the beach, except an occasional dog walker. Luckily, the breeze was quite mild and the air warmed up some as they proceeded. They talked about their lives and interests. They had a lot in common in that they both were politically liberal and cared profoundly about the environment.

Being that Phoebe had been married and had been in love before, Isaiah a bit jealous over her dead husband, asked her. "What was it like to be married to Daniel? Did you want children with him? I am not sure why I'm asking that. If you don't want to talk about that, I understand. I've never wanted children before, but being with you, I started to think, already last night, that maybe I do."

Before Phoebe had a chance to answer him, a rather large malamute ran up to Isaiah and rubbed its nose up against his pants. Isaiah bent over and petted the pooch, which made some responsive singing sounds and wagged its tail enthusiastically. The dog's owner came up to them. She was a very pretty and tall blond woman about their age.

"Abby usually doesn't take to strangers, but it appears that you are singular. My name is Dannie, and you have already met Abby."

Phoebe and Isaiah introduced themselves.

"Abby is such a beautiful malamute. How do you keep her coat so shiny in all this sand?" Isaiah asked.

"We just left home. I live in that house over there, and I hose her down frequently. I also give her egg yolks, and that seems to make her fur shiny. Again, I am impressed that you know that she is a malamute," Dannie stated.

"Isaiah works and befriends wolves, and all dogs seem to love him too. He has been able to name every dog we have seen so far, and most of them come up to greet him too, which isn't really all that many, because we just met yesterday," Phoebe confided.

"The way the two of you are together, I thought you must have been together for a good while. There is a light emanating from you that shines brightly. I am into the healing arts and have the ability to pick up things in that regard more than most. Your light is very bright, so I wouldn't be surprised if many people, who are not too self obsessed, would notice it," Dannie related.

"Wow, that is truly amazing. I think most folks are too into their own crap to notice, but thanks for your observation. Are you in a relationship as well. I can't tell by looking at you, but you are a beautiful woman, and oh it's none of our business," Phoebe said.

"No, I like real conversations rather than common clichés, and that is a legitimate question. Actually, I have been concentrating on my work, and Abby is my closest relationship now. I've had numerous relationships with boys and men, and even an occasional woman," as she winked at Phoebe, tossing her long blond hair over her head, "but nothing now," Dannie related.

Abby did not want Isaiah to leave just yet, and got Isaiah to play with her, while the girls chatted some more. Finally Dannie collared her dog and told her to let these people have some time alone. The canine would have none of that.

Phoebe spoke up, "Why don't you come along with us and show us the sights here at your beach?"

"I'd love to, or we'd love to, but I know that you two are into a romantic walk now, and we'd just be in the way. Why don't you two drop by my house after your walk is over, and we can talk a bit more, and exchange texting information, etc." Dannie said, as she dragged her big doggy in the opposite direction.

"Huh, that sure was different," Phoebe said to Isaiah, as they continued toward the shoreline. "What did you think of that?"

"I liked her. She was a real and genuine person, and Abby and I bonded very quickly too, a fine pooch," Isaiah responded.

"She is very beautiful too, isn't she?" Phoebe asked.

"She is a very beautiful dog, and Dannie wasn't bad either," Isaiah teased.

They were by a tide pool and Phoebe dipped her hands in and splashed Isaiah on his face with the cool water. He grabbed her by her shoulders and pulled her into his arms and kissed her firmly on her lips. The kiss lasted for over a minute and stirred up those earlier feelings and sensations that they had.

"I guess you respond positively to being splashed. I will have to remember that," Phoebe said, with a gentle yet flirtatious voice, and her adoring eyes gazing at her beloved new friend.

Both Isaiah and Phoebe were naturalists at heart. They walked among the tide pools and they pointed out to each other some of the fauna that were living or visiting, including: mussels, snails, crabs, limpets and even barnacles. Isaiah also pointed out the common flora including: Sea Lettuce, Sea Cabbage, Sea Moss, Rockweed, and a bunch of different types of kelp.

Once it warmed up a bit more they removed their sneakers, pulled up the bottom of their pants, and walked at the edge of the shore where the tide had just about finished its ebb phase. They knew they had a couple of hours before they had to get back to the wider beach. The water was quite chilly, especially at first, but they walked quickly, and the icy water seemed to feel warmer as they proceeded. They took turns being the closest to the water's edge. Isaiah noticed that Phoebe had really sexy ankles and calves. Phoebe noticed that Isaiah had really strong and muscular legs too, and they both fantasized about having fun in the future with those gams.

Isaiah spoke up first, "I have been admiring your legs and feet, Phoebe. They are really sensual, and they turn me on, watching you walk."

"That's funny, because I've been admiring your strong calves as well since you rolled up your pants. I was fantasizing how much fun it would be to play with them and touch them sensually."

They stopped and hugged each other again, feeling each other's embrace rippling through their bodies like an inescapable avalanche. They started kissing again, as they had earlier in the truck. Their lips were moist and hungry for action. The crescendo was building, as Isaiah penetrated Phoebe's opening with his tongue, softly yet decisively probing her receptive mouth, while she caught his tongue with her desirous tongue, and retaliated and escalated the sensation with thrusts of her own. They were getting real turned on, barely hearing the sound of the waves. While they were in the throes of this intense erotic pleasure, a large wave rolled in and rode up above their knees, ending the loving embrace of the two lovers, as Phoebe squealed, and Isaiah laughed They both ran away from the water's edge, joyous, laughing, but a bit wet.

"I guess Mother Nature didn't want us to be too ecstatic, but that surely was a great kiss," Phoebe said, as they walked back to Dannie's house. It was an older house, but looked clean, kept up, and had nice foliage and spring flowers around it. They were about to knock at the door when Dannie opened it. Abby jumped out and enthusiastically nuzzled Isaiah.

"Welcome to my humble abode. Please come on in," Dannie politely yet authoritatively stated.

They entered with Abby still pressing up affectionately against Isaiah's legs. Phoebe noticed the numerous beautiful paintings on many of the walls, and said, "I wouldn't call this place humble. It is more like a museum. These paintings are so colorful and beautiful. They look like they were painted by the same artist. I'm a bit of an art aficionado and I'd love to meet the artist."

"Well, you already have. I painted every one of these. I guess I'm a bit of a narcissist, hanging up only my own paintings, but they are like children to me, and I have a difficult time selling them, even though there have been numerous offers for many of them."

"They really are fantastic," Isaiah and Phoebe said at the same time, as they looked at each other, and noticed that they were both giggling, which had all three of them giggle some more.

"They remind me of Marc Chagall's works, but totally your own style. They remind me of a cross between Chagall, and some of the impressionists, such as Van Gogh. I have a couple of Chagall's prints in my home," Phoebe added.

"You do have a good eye. I always loved Chagall's colors and Van Gogh's imagination. When I look at the two of you together I visualize two warm entities blending together and becoming one large colorful, compassionate creation spreading out and filling the void. I think you two have given me an inspiration for my next painting," Dannie related.

"That is exciting. I'd love to see that," Phoebe continued. "What is the inspiration for that painting over there with the birds flying out of the ocean that looks like it is a brain?"

"I had this dream where I was taken to the underworld of some Olympian Gods or something like that, to go to this party with all kinds of animals and creatures. When the party broke up, everyone dispersed into different directions and I turned into a colorful bird, and flew with this magnificent flock of vibrantly tinted birds in an amazing maneuver towards the sky and the sun. I looked the birds up on the Internet after I woke up, and they were *Scarlet Tanagers* and *Paradise Tanagers,* a small songbird of the Amazon River basin. They signify patience with anticipation. I just had to paint that beautiful dream memory, and started the painting that same day."

"That is a wonderful story, and a fantastic painting indeed. I like flying dreams. I think I must have been a bird in some past life. I am really drawn to your paintings," Phoebe complimented, and then asked to use the bathroom. There were a couple of beautiful flower paintings behind glass frames in the bathroom that Phoebe thought marvelous.

Meanwhile, Abby had taken to sitting right at the feet of Isaiah, which Phoebe noticed upon returning. He was giving Dannie a little malamute lesson.

"Did you know that malamutes were one of the earliest evolutionary branches when wolves evolved into dogs? They are real pack dogs and they are not as puppyish once they grow up, as most domesticated dogs are. They are considered a natural breed, as their genetics were not interfered with by humans. They had the quality of being able to pull sleds, and so were left alone to do just that. They are pack oriented, as wolves are. You can still get all kinds of personalities, and Abby here is gentle and kind compared to many of the malamutes that I saw in Alaska."

"That's interesting," Dannie responded. "I sure like the two of you, and I don't like that many people. Most of my friends are scattered across the country and even are living in other countries. I hope that you come back and visit soon. I hope you don't mind my being so blunt, but I am very turned on by the two of you, and wouldn't mind seeing something develop in that regard."

"I will take that as a compliment and appreciate your candor," Phoebe answered, with a glint in her eye. "As we mentioned, Isaiah and I just met yesterday, and we haven't even gone to bed yet, so to add on someone else, though as enticing as you are, is a bit premature. Perhaps in time, but we will have to discuss this between us first, and I don't think it will be imminent, but who knows."

"Well, as long as you think I am enticing, then I think that I can live with that," Dannie teased and added. "Let's stay in contact and if things change, let me know, and if they don't, I still hope we can all be friends."

Isaiah said, "I promised Phoebe that I'd take her to brunch this morning. It's time that we headed there before it gets too busy. We appreciate your friendliness and your honesty. I hope we get to see you again too, as you truly are enticing and talented. I don't live in this area, but with Phoebe and my mother down here, I will be sure to be back before too long."

Chapter 8
Phoebe Isaiah

"Holy moly Phoebe, that was intense," Isaiah said after he and Phoebe departed from Dannie and Abby with some friendly hugs, petting Abby, and genial good byes, but not the same way as the sexual hugs that they had earlier with each other. Abby wanted to leave with them, as they opened the door, but Dannie called her back and the pooch let them leave without further interruption.

"Yes, I agree. That was something else. That Dannie sure is a powerfully willed woman. I liked her, her paintings are really gorgeous too, but she was a bit scary at times with her bluntness. I am glad that we were on the same page. I don't think that I could have resisted her advances without you at my side," Phoebe stated, once they had gotten back in the pickup.

"I totally agree, Isaiah responded. She is different from anyone that I have ever met for sure; tantalizing and assertive. I sure liked Abby. A person who has such a terrific dog, especially a malamute, must be doing something right."

"I didn't really feel her turn-on like we had together on the beach. I'm still feeling a bit on overwhelm and feel kind of out of my body. There was just too much going on. I've been here many times before and always admired that house. I'm glad we got to check it out," Isaiah stated.

"I think that she is a very sexual woman, but she probably hasn't gotten off for some time, and her sexual tumescence is killing her turn-on. She really could use a tumble in the hay, some heavy pressure maybe, but we weren't in a place to provide that for her," Phoebe explained. "I have taken some sensual and tantric classes, and she could definitely benefit from something like that. Anyhow, it feels good to be just the two of us again. I'm hungry and I bet you are too."

"It's less than fifteen minutes from here. I'll drive fast. I know the owner and she will take good care of us," Isaiah avowed.

They both were quiet and slowed down their breathing, so that they fell back into their bodies by the time Isaiah pulled up off the road into one of the last remaining spaces at the *Olema Bistro*. As soon as Isaiah got out of the truck, 2 large dogs came up to him, wagging their tales quickly in a back and forth motion of happy excitement, and started licking his hands.

"Romulus and Remus, I am glad to see the two of you as well," Isaiah proclaimed, as the dogs continued their licking. "This is Phoebe," Isaiah whispered to the dogs. Remus gave Phoebe a few licks too, and then Romulus did as well, and then both went back to greet Isaiah some more.

A dark haired woman with some gray showing, probably in her fifties, with her hair tied back in a tight pony tail, came out after the dogs to see why they left the building. She saw Isaiah and immediately came over to greet him too, without the licking.

"I couldn't figure out why the boys sprinted out so quickly, but now I realize why. It's good to see you Isaiah. It's been over a year, hasn't it? And who is this beautiful woman that you have brought with you?" Adele winked, as she held out her hand to welcome Phoebe.

"I'm Phoebe, and you must be Adele. Isaiah told me how nice you have been to him and how great the brunches are here. I'm ready to confirm his gastro-recommendation."

"Come on in then." Adele stated, then shouted, "Romulus, Remus, let Isaiah be, and let them get some brunch. You two already ate."

The dogs let Isaiah and Phoebe pass on into the restaurant after getting one last lick each on Isaiah's hands. Adele gave them a special table in this upstairs' small nook area that looked out over the distant ocean. Isaiah went to wash his hands. Adele sat down with Phoebe.

"Isaiah and I go back a long ways. His mom Kenisha actually was my nurse when I had my two kids back in the late 80's at Marin General. Kenisha had Isaiah about a year later, so I've known him practically his entire life. They used to come here all the time when he was small, and he'd run around with my brats. We don't see each other too often anymore, but think of them as family. How did the two of you meet Phoebe; you also look awfully familiar, like I've seen you on TV or something?"

"Actually, we just met yesterday at a coffee shop, but really hit it off quickly. I used to be on the *World News* on *ABC*, so you probably saw me there."

"You are Phoebe Granger. You were married to Daniel Granger, who was my favorite news reporter. That was horrible what happened to him. I am so sorry for you. I'm glad that you have moved on. My husband died about ten years ago in a boating accident off the coast here. I know how hard it is to lose your mate."

"Thank you, yes, Daniel was a great man. It has taken me these past few years to start really getting back to living again. Yesterday, when I woke up, I felt that I was ready for a new great relationship for the first time, and Isaiah just happened to walk by me a few hours later. I thought he was so cute, and I was immediately attracted to his presence."

"He is a good one, that boy. No one has really gotten their hooks into him, but the way he looks at you, I can tell that he has already changed. Good for you, I say. You are still young and beautiful, and you deserve a second chance with someone special."

"Thanks, I appreciate that, Adele. My old friend told me this morning that I deserve someone special too, but I told her that deserving it doesn't make it so. I figure I conjured Isaiah up," Phoebe replied, and then asked, "I see that colorful painting over there," pointing toward the wall at the other side of the room. "It looks like it was painted by this woman Dannie that we met this morning at the beach?"

"You are right. She hates selling her babies, as she calls them, but I finally wore her down, and she sold it to me. It wasn't cheap, but it is so beautiful," Adele bragged.

"I know, I loved all her stuff. Her dog came up to Isaiah; made a big fuss over him of course, and she invited us inside her home after we talked, so I got to see her beautiful work covering all the wall space of her house."

"She's a good person that Dannie is, a bit intense, but she has a big heart. She comes here regularly. I also knew her family well. They've had that house at the beach for three generations now. Her parents moved to assisted living a few years back. Her dad had a heart attack and a stroke, and had a difficult time getting around. Her mom is a painter too, not as good as her daughter, but not bad."

"You know a lot of people, don't you?" Phoebe asked rhetorically.

Adele answered anyhow, "You have to in my business, plus I love gossip. What do Jewish people call it, a yenta, I think?"

"Yes, yenta is the word, though I think you are just a savvy business woman. I am part Jewish, my mom is Jewish, though my dad isn't. He owns a beer making establishment. I bet you know him as well?" Phoebe inquired, as Isaiah came back from the restroom.

"I'm glad that you two are hitting it off. What are you discussing?" Isaiah asked, as he sat down.

"Besides you," Adele winked at him. "I was just about to ask Phoebe, what her dad's name is, and what his business is called."

"It's Phillips, Dave Phillips and the *Phillips Brewery,*" Phoebe responded.

"Of course I know Dave. We can't get enough of his beer. Practically all my beer drinking customers love his craft beer. He is quite the artist," Adele exclaimed.

"I'll be sure to tell him that. He would love the praise, being a Leo and all that. Not that I believe in astrology, but I think Leos do." Phoebe remarked.

"That's funny, I'm a Leo and I think that astrology is kind of right on," Adele responded. "Maybe you can get him to let me have more of his beer, being that we are both Leos. So I know you are both hungry, so enough chitchat. What can I have them bring you to eat?"

"Their omelets are great here. I like the Mitake mushroom, avocado, sautéed arugula with herbs, and Gruyere cheese," Isaiah recommended.

"That sounds great. I'll take one of those, plus some crispy bacon, and crispy fried sweet potatoes, with a side of toasted sourdough bread, and a cup of coffee," Phoebe hungrily ordered.

"Wow, that is exactly what I'll have too. I see we both are crispy fans, maybe the coffee doesn't have to be that crispy, and we are both hungry," Isaiah chortled.

Adele left to have their order filled. Phoebe pointed out the Dannie painting on the wall.

"She is quite the painter. I guess she is following us, or maybe we are following her." Isaiah laughed. "I thought she didn't sell her paintings," he added.

"That is what I thought too, but Adele told me that she was very persuasive, which I heartily believe from just meeting her, and that she paid Dannie a good sum to boot," Phoebe responded.

The food arrived in no time, and the conversation stopped, as they both ate voraciously.

"You remind me of how a wolf eats when it's hungry," Isaiah teased, after they both had downed a good portion of their large and very tasty meals.

"I was really starving and this cuisine is totally delicious. You went with me toe to toe, or bite to bite, so I didn't feel embarrassed by scarfing it down, Mr. Wolf," Phoebe retaliated, then putting another piece of bacon in her mouth and making loud crunching sounds.

They finished eating and supping on a second cup of Joe with a piece of freshly baked coffee cake that the waitress brought out, that was on the house. They walked back downstairs, a few pounds heavier, said good bye, plus expressing their appreciation for the fine dining experience to Adele. Of course Isaiah had to say good bye to Romulus and Remus before getting back in his truck.

Chapter 9
Phoebe Isaiah

"I really am having the best day. Thank you for taking me to these wonderful places Isaiah," Phoebe acknowledged, as they headed back inland enjoying the scenic ride, a beautiful drive alongside *Samuel P. Taylor State Park* and lots of large redwoods.

Phoebe asked, "What are you going to do this afternoon?"

"Well, I have to drive back north before it gets too late. Did you have anything in mind?" Isaiah answered and asked.

Phoebe wondered how direct she should be. She really wanted Isaiah to make her an offer, and then to make outrageous love to her. She was still fearful that if she was too aggressive and made him the offer that she would scare him off. She also knew that she was more experienced than he was, and if she didn't say something that she could let a grand opportunity slip away. She said nothing at first, giving Isaiah the time to come up with the suggestion.

Isaiah had checked off many of the boxes that Phoebe had put on her relationship list, including: handsome, tall, smart, funny, enjoys similar foods, good kisser and hugger, smells good, generous, humorous, strong, spiritual, a good relationship with his mother, likes dogs (he got a special bonus for that category or dogegory she punned to herself), responds to her whims, well groomed, neat enough, adventurous, etc. She still hadn't crossed off the boxes for sexual prowess and sleep-ability.

"I was just wondering what time you had to leave, that's all, and also to let you know that I had a wonderful time with you today, even though you said that I scarfed my food down like a wolf. I know how much you like wolves, so I took it as a term of endearment," Phoebe hedged her bet.

"This is more intimate time than I have spent with anyone in a long while, perhaps my entire life. I really don't want it to end either. Would you like to continue hanging out with me this afternoon until I take off?" Isaiah finally asked, as Phoebe's heart skipped a beat and her eyes glimmered in gratitude to Cupid or whatever entity that had put them together.

"Yes, I'd like that very much," Phoebe quickly replied, to reward Isaiah for making the correct response. She wanted to take advantage of his forthcoming overture towards her. She had read that in relationships, one of the two people had the foot on the accelerator, while the other party had the foot on the brakes. She also knew that often the chemistry between two people in the beginning of a relationship was such that both parties had their feet on the accelerator.

Phoebe offered, "I think it would be great if you would take me home and then perhaps you could come upstairs for a cup of coffee or tea or whatever."

Normally Isaiah would not have picked up so quickly on a woman's desires, but he could feel the engorgement in his loins and he quickly responded. "Yes, that would be fantastic."

The rest of the drive was filled with pheromones or sexual signals that were emanating from Phoebe that kept Isaiah and herself turned on and feeling very much alive. He was able to drive safely in spite of feeling like stopping the vehicle several times, and taking Phoebe in the back seat. Phoebe was thrilled with how she had manifested this whole outing and was tingling all over. They arrived at Phoebe's home a little past one.

Isaiah and Phoebe both got out of the vehicle. They both took deep breaths. The air was fresh. They then quickly walked over to each other and wrapped their arms around the other's body and embraced. This was a full body embrace. Phoebe could feel the firmness of Isaiah and she could feel the wetness in hers. He smelled her hair and kissed her neck and she felt like she was melting into bliss.

"You feel so wonderful in my arms and pressing against my thighs," Phoebe exclaimed. "I think we should take this pleasurable encirclement inside, before we entertain the neighbors too much."

"You make me feel so alive and joyful. Being close to you like this is the best place to be in the whole world," Isaiah remarked, before letting Phoebe out of his sizzling grasp.

They held hands walking into her townhouse. Once inside Phoebe's home, they pulled each other very close, so that they could kiss and feel their bodies pressed up together again. There was no ocean wave this time to interrupt them, just waves of pleasure to enhance their feelings, as they slowly probed each other's lips with fine attention. Phoebe was pressing her thigh against his member, and she could feel how hard he had responded to her. She was slowly moving him toward her bedroom in a slow passionate dance to the beating of their hearts.

Then the home-phone rang. It was Daniel's younger sister Bella, whose voice came from the answering machine. "I'm on my way over to see you. I should be there in about fifteen minutes. I need to talk to you badly. I am going through a difficult time, and you are the only person who I know, who can help me. I tried calling you on your cell, but you had it turned off. I hope you are home, because otherwise I don't know what I will do. Hopefully, I will see you soon."

"Shit!" Phoebe exclaimed. "We always get interrupted when we are so high, maybe that's a good thing, maybe. I have to get into agreement. It's fun in some way going up and up and then having the rug pulled from under you. It's a real roller coaster ride and we didn't get hurt."

Isaiah knew that he had to leave. It was probably time for him to head back north anyhow. He had to say goodbye to his mom and pick up his stuff there. He knew in his heart of hearts that he would be seeing Phoebe again. He was pretty sure of that, if it was meant to be. Isaiah really wished for more of Phoebe, and he would do his best to make sure that came to fruition, and then it would happen.

"I think it best if I leave now. It has been special and wonderful spending the day with you Phoebe, and I hope that we can see each other soon," Isaiah lovingly stated.

Phoebe responded longingly, "You are right. You have to leave. I wanted you to know that you are the best thing that has happened to me in a very long time, and if you want, maybe I can come up and visit you soon. I probably can even get a magazine such as *National Geographic* to let me do a story on your wolves. I'll walk you out to your car and wait for Bella. Bella is very beautiful and still very young. I have strong maternal or sisterly feelings for her because she is Daniel's only sister, and he would want me to help her, but she lives her life as if she was the center of the universe."

Isaiah kissed Phoebe on her forehead, told her that she was a kind and loving person, that he had a fantastic time, and hoped they could start off again where they left off. He squeezed her hand tenderly, but for the time being, their erotic dance was postponed once again.

Chapter 10
Bella

Jehovah is my witness, Isaiah thought to himself, something his mother always said. *Man, I like Phoebe. This Bella looks like trouble incarnated in those short shorts.* Bella drove up, as Isaiah got into his truck. He could make out a very cute blond woman get out of her car. Isaiah thought that she still seemed more of a girl or pre-woman than a full fledged woman. Bella looked to be around 20 years old. She had a very nice figure, and he blessed her with his compassion, in order not to be upset with her interrupting his interlude with Phoebe. She didn't seem to notice him, as she strode toward the house. Phoebe called to her, and they went inside together after a short hug. Isaiah took off in his truck, once they disappeared into the building.

Phoebe had just a couple of minutes from when Isaiah left to forgive Bella for her untimely intrusion. She was no longer seething, but she wasn't totally placid yet either. The girls hugged each other, more of a teepee hug than the full body hug she was just involved in with Isaiah.

"So what is it that you have that is so vital that you have to see me about so urgently?" Phoebe asked in as pleasant a voice as she could muster.

"I'm so glad that you are here. I was just with my boyfriend and found out that he was seeing another woman behind my back. I confronted him with my knowledge and he at first denied it, but then I finally got him to admit that he had seen someone else," Bella responded in a state of intense emotion.

"Oh dear, that is a tough one. This was that guy Randy who I met at your parent's Thanksgiving last year? To tell you the truth I thought he wasn't good enough for you then," Phoebe stated, serving Bella some coffee and some calming herbal tea for herself.

"No, no," Bella replied. Randy and I broke up around Christmas. This is a new guy I just met at school. His name is Jamison. He is a graduate student in my field, and I really liked him so much. I thought that we were perfect for each other. We were seeing each other for over a month already. He had a girlfriend before we got together. They broke up, but then he saw her again. I found their texts to each other on his phone, while he spent the night with me last night. I told him to leave. I really wanted him to beg for my forgiveness, but he left. What do you think I should do?" Bella asked with tears in her eyes."

"Oh Bella, I think you are fortunate that he left and did not beg for your forgiveness, cause you probably would have given it to him. I think that for a guy to see his ex is not the worst thing in the world, but it would have been better if he was up front about it, and at least admitted it when you first confronted him. People do lie when confronted however, because one of the main reasons to lie is to avoid punishment. The other main reason is to impress, but he wasn't doing that. He was afraid that you would punish him, and he is right of course for thinking that. The ball is really in your hands now. If you want to see him again then you can state the boundaries that are permitted and what will not be allowed. It is all about good communications. If you don't think that you can trust him anymore, then it probably is time to move on. As I said, you have the ball in your court, and you hold the best cards, to use a couple of clichés. You are in an advantageous position."

"I like that, being in the advantageous position. I feel better already. You are so smart Phoebe. I knew that you could help me. I also have been thinking about having an affair with my philosophy professor. He is really cute and I can tell that I turn him on. He stares at me all the time in my class. I know that you and Daniel were in a similar circumstance. Do you think that I should pursue my professor?" Bella asked, as if she had already forgotten about her last lover.

Phoebe thought to herself. *I can't believe I fell for Bella's psychodrama and let Isaiah go so easily. I am either a big fool, or too kindhearted, or both.* "When I met Daniel, it was love at first sight for both of us. We both knew it right away, yet still kept an appropriate distance for propriety sake. I don't know how your professor feels, but I would make sure that he feels the same way as you do, and that you feel the same way in a month or two, or even next week," Phoebe answered, hoping against great odds to have Bella understand that the entire world doesn't only spin around her self-centered axis.

"I know that Rod, that's the professor's name, is into me by the way he looks at me. I'm sure that he will ask me out and I will respond affirmatively. I know you and my brother were more surreptitious, but I think that times have changed and one has to be themselves, and not worry what anyone else thinks, or what society holds as proper," Bella said, rebuffing Phoebe's attempt at teaching her.

"So Phoebe what have you been doing for fun?" Bella uncharacteristically asked, probably wanting to end the professor conversation more than really caring what Phoebe was doing.

"I just had the best time since Daniel died, with a new guy I just met yesterday. We went to *Bolinas Beach* for a walk and then out for a delicious brunch at the *Olema Bistro*. He works for the *California Fish and Game Agency,* and specializes in the maintenance of wolves," Phoebe responded, very much enjoying the sensation that talking about Isaiah brought her.

"That's nice, I had a boyfriend my first year in college who wanted to become involved with cleaning up the ocean and reestablishing fish that were endangered and disappearing. I realized that he was more interested in fish than in me, so I quickly dropped him. I think you can do better than getting involved with a 'wolf' man, but I'm glad you had fun Phoebe," Bella said, focusing the attention back on Bella, where it usually was. "I believe that I will talk to Rod after class next week, after just thinking about it" Bella asserted.

Phoebe had enough of Bella for the time being. She momentarily got pissed off again when Bella denigrated Isaiah, but forgave her again, and just wanted her to leave. She politely told Bella that she had work to do, but she really wanted to talk to her friend Rachel about Isaiah. Bella left to Phoebe's relief, though she would have preferred to have some more time with Phoebe, talking about herself.

The phone rang as soon as Bella departed. "Hi Phoebe," it was Rachel.

"Wow, I was just about to call you. What's up Rache?"

"Nothing with me, but I was curious how your date with Isaiah went, and if he has a last name yet?" Rachel inquired.

"That is why I was calling you, or almost calling you. It was better than I had hoped for. We kissed and hugged often, a great kisser, I might add. I was getting really turned on a number of occasions, and so was he. I could really feel him hard against me on several body hugs. He is funny, kind, and crosses off almost all the boxes of my most important characteristics for a lover checklist. We almost went to bed a little while ago. We came back from the beach and were madly kissing and feeling each other up when my sister in law Bella interrupted, and put the kibosh on my erotic feelings for the moment. He had to go back north anyhow, and this way we get to long for each other even more. His last name is Williams, so you might find a bunch of folks with that name, but probably only one who works for *California Fish and Wildlife.* Thanks, but I don't think it's necessary to investigate Isaiah, and I'd actually prefer you didn't, because nothing you could say would change my mind anyhow," Phoebe stated to her friend.

"Got it. I won't if you don't want me to. I'm probably too paranoid anyway, and he certainly sounds like a keeper. He makes you happy already. I mean you are happy around him, and even when thinking about him, and as long as you continue to feel that way about him, I whole heartedly approve," Rachel remarked.

"We also met a couple of interesting people on our morning adventure. There was this very pretty woman who had a dog that was all over Isaiah. You won't believe how quickly and demonstrably dogs take to him. It's not anything visible on his part, but every dog that we have come across seems to fall in love with him and give him their full respect immediately. It's uncanny. It is like he has a dog whistle that only they can hear. I guess I can hear it too," Phoebe and Rachel both laughed.

"Anyhow, the dog's owner has a nice home, right overlooking the beach, and invited us in. She kind of made some sensual advances to the both of us. I was tempted, but since Isaiah and I have not been to bed yet, it would have been too early in our relationship, but I was intrigued. She is an artist and has many really beautiful paintings in her home that she created. I mean they were really top notch, museum worthy. The other person I met was an old friend of Isaiah's who owns the bistro near the beach. She knows my dad and the food there was amazing too," Phoebe said, remembering the wonderful time she had had earlier in the day, though it already seemed like a long time ago.

"I am so happy for you," Rachel said. "So how are you going to reel him in, with his own rod?" Rachel guffawed, using the metaphor of part of the name that Isaiah worked for.

"I think he already is reeled in, as you put it. I don't have to do anything, but be myself. He likes me for who I am. He even had a crush on my TV personality when I was a TV reporter on *ABC*. I feel turned on when I'm with him, even just thinking about him, more than with Daniel, whom you know I adored. I'm sure the lust will wear off eventually, but I like his personality, his openness, and his not needing to be the center of attention all the time, except maybe with those canines." Phoebe responded.

"Okay, so what is next? Are you going to go visit him in the wilderness? Do you think your mother will approve of him? You know how prejudice she is, especially about societal class, and him being a black guy to boot," Rachel questioned.

"My mother will just have to accept whomever I desire, king or pawn, black or white. Besides, this will give her an opportunity to become a better human being. It is time she gave up her old negative prejudices and come live in this century. If she can't, then I still have my dad and Lori, who will accept Isaiah right away. They are more fun to be around anyhow. And yes, I will go visit Isaiah as soon as I can, in a castle or in a shack, or wherever he lives," Phoebe answered convincingly.

"Thanks for the update Pheobes. You are the best. Love you," as the phone call ended.

The phone rang again. This time Isaiah spoke first. "Are you all right Phoebe? Is your sister okay? It seemed we were up there in the clouds together, and then suddenly I was back on the ground by myself."

Phoebe responded, "Yes, everything is fine. I'm really sorry that we had to end it so abruptly. I'm glad you are calling me, because I've been thinking and talking about you since you left, first with Bella and then my old friend Rachel in New York. I gave you a 5 star review to both of them, though Bella who is a wannabe diva did not accept my description of you as whole heartedly as Rachel. Bella pays little attention to anyone else, other than herself, and her urgency for seeing me was not really that urgent or important either. Thanks for understanding. She still is Daniel's little sister, and I do have a maternal or sisterly attitude toward her, although not every mother has to love their child. Rachel was thrilled for me, and wants to know about you some more, once we get together again, hint hint."

"I'm glad that everyone is okay. I'd love for you to visit. You can visit me anytime. That fills me with sensation again. I went from feeling so high in your foyer to hardly feeling anything since we parted. My dwellings don't resemble a 5 star resort, but I can show you some natural habitats away from civilization that are even more rewarding in many respects," Isaiah added.

"I've been to plenty of 5 star places, and many of them are highly overrated. The important thing is to be with someone that you love and feel joyful around, and so far you are that 5 star person, as I told Rachel and Bella. I know it's kind of early in a relationship to talk about love, but when you feel something as strongly as I do for you, then I think not expressing it would be a sin," Phoebe confidently confessed.

Isaiah responded," Well, not really ever having felt this way before, I am totally new to these sensations, but they obviously feel rather wonderful. I find you so charming, beautiful, and titillating. I am so intoxicated by your essence, even your voice now on the phone takes me to another level. I want to get to know you even better, and to enjoy you on your journey, and for us to be as happy and adventurous as we can."

"Listen to us. We are like a couple of teenagers in love for the first time. Please drive safely Isaiah, don't let me distract you from the road."

"If I could drive safely with you sitting next to me feeling the way I did, I think I should be able to handle the wheel right now. Maybe you have felt this way before, but for me it is a totally new emotion, and I rather like it. I don't know how long these sensations will last, but let's enjoy them while we have them, don't you think?" Isaiah asked.

"Of course, being present, and appreciating whatever comes my way, is my main mantra. When it is pleasure and fun like I am having with you, that makes it easier. I am not going to take you or any of these pleasant sensations for granted. I think the more joy we can entertain in our daily observations and interpretations, the more pleasure and fun will also come our way," Phoebe reverently remarked.

"That's a lovely viewpoint to entertain. I don't think that I am as spiritually evolved as you are, but I have been working at it lately. I still get pissed off when one of my wolves is poisoned or killed. I don't like it when unfair things happen to defenseless animals or even to people. I'd like to learn how to get into agreement with my outrage, yet still be an effective advocate for what caused the outrage to begin with," Isaiah responded.

"That is a noble goal. I think the outrage is our natural response to an unwanted and selected causality, and to want to do something about it is a positive enlightened view. The trick is to let it go in your mind so that you don't dwell on the negativity and the suffering that only you can create and maintain. Like they say, *I care, but I don't mind*. Knowing you, even for the short time that I do, I am sure you are being an effective advocate for those creatures who you care about," Phoebe said, bringing gentle tears to both their eyes.

"Here I am pontificating, and it's only recently that I've gotten some healing from the wound of losing my husband.

I am still a work in progress. I am so glad that you came around now and not earlier, because I was not ready for a relationship then, and probably not until that morning that I met you," Phoebe added.

"Wow, I guess I had good timing there. Sure wouldn't want to have met you and been rejected before I got a chance to demonstrate my wonderfulness to you," Isaiah joked.

"Me too," Phoebe interjected. "Please call me again shortly, or I'll call you. I'm going to arrange to visit you real soon. Meanwhile let's stay in good communications, and enjoy the opportunity of longing for each other, my love."

"That sounds awesome. I look forward to hearing from you, and definitely will be longing for you until you do, my love," Isaiah emoted, repeating Phoebe's declaration; putting his attention back on the highway that had all of a sudden gotten crowded.

Chapter 11
Isaiah Wolves Stephanie

Keeping to his schedule, Isaiah stopped off quickly at his mom's place to pick up his stuff and give her a hug. She could tell that he was happy and told him that she was glad that he had found somebody that he liked.

"You're the best mom. I love you dearly," Isaiah said, as he promptly took off for the wilderness. Isaiah arrived back at his cabin in the woods late at night and had to get up early the next day. He had plenty of energy, and he woke up without the alarm clock. Before starting his regular outdoor work on Monday, Isaiah had to check in at the field office in Redding. It was a small office, but the two women working there seemed to take more notice of Isaiah than usual. Usually they hardly spoke with him, except to give him any updates that were necessary for him to have. Nora, a pretty black woman about his age, told him how he seemed different from usual. She asked him out for some coffee before he headed back out to the wilderness.

Isaiah accepted. He thought a coffee would hit the spot before going back out in the field. He had the fleeting thought that he was somehow betraying Phoebe by going for coffee with another woman, but quieted his guilt with the fact that he wanted coffee, and he was not interested in Nora as relationship material, plus he doubted that she had any real interest in him either.

He was wrong. Nora complimented him for the way he dressed, and how she always found him attractive, and even more so today. She looked at him more directly than she ever had before. He could feel a little turn-on coming from her, though it was hedged in her doubt, so was not hitting its mark full on.

"I don't know what it is about you Isaiah, but you have a gleam in your eye that I never really noticed before. Did you get some this weekend when you went home?" Nora frankly asked.

"I did meet someone while I was in Marin. We didn't have sex, if that is what you are referring to, but we did hit it off quite intensely. I do hope to see her again," Isaiah answered truthfully.

"Good for you Isaiah. you must have fallen for her strongly, for you have that taken look about you that makes you more attractive. I once read in a relationship book how men who are single are not very appealing to women, but once they are picked by a woman that they like, she gets her juices all over him, so to speak, and he then becomes way more appealing to other women. It is similar to when people are hungry, and looking for a restaurant to eat in, but won't go into an empty restaurant, but if the restaurant is full, they will wait for hours to get in. Truthfully, I was going to ask you out just now, but I think that ship has already sailed," Nora shrugged.

"Hmm, I appreciate your honesty, and I've never heard that analogy before. It makes a lot of sense though," Isaiah responded. "To be honest with you, last week I would have jumped at the chance to go out with you. Now however, I feel that would be a betrayal of this new relationship I find myself in. I know I may be reading too much into such a new connection, but my mother and grandmother both taught me to not to be a womanizer, and only be intimate with one person at a time."

"I respect you even more now. You were brought up properly. I had two years to make my move, and missed my chance. Your new friend must be very special to get her hooks into you so effectively, quickly, and apparently lovingly; with no one there eating at your restaurant," Nora said jokingly.

Isaiah drove back to the area, close to his cabin, where the wolf pack that he was following had their den and their rendezvous site, which was used as a staging area for their hunt, usually at dusk, and a safe place to leave their pups with a pup sitter, usually one of the younger members of the pack. Isaiah had a yurt tent even nearer to this area, and slept out with the wolves on occasion.

The 7 wolves in the pack were all hanging out together. The 3 yearlings, Huey, Dooey, and Looey were playing with their former pup sitter that Isaiah called Pippa. She had relieved her sister, the alpha female that Isaiah named Rebecca the previous spring and summer when Rebecca had had enough mothering. Rebecca and the alpha male that Isaiah named Barack, and Barack's brother Antonio were dozing peacefully, but woke up when he walked towards them. They all wagged their tales and greeted him affectionately. Isaiah let them lick his hands and also scolded them in a tender friendly fashion for recently consuming some livestock. It was almost spring, the time of the year to birth a litter, and Rebecca was pregnant again, and the pups were due in a few weeks. The gestation time is only 2 months, and pups are born blind, and only can live off their mother's milk for the first few weeks. A couple of months after the initial suckling period, the pups can eat some solid food, but their jaws are not strong enough yet to chew raw meat on their own, so the older members of the pack regurgitate their meals after predigesting it partially. Isaiah thought that it was time to give Huey, Dooey, and Looey some new names, as they had outgrown their old ones.

It seemed that some sheep DNA had shown up in more than one of the scats that Isaiah had sent the week before to the office for analysis. He was informed of the results this morning at the office. He knew that wolves did not attack livestock as often as rancher's claimed, but this happened to be one of those cases. He also knew that it was probably from the sheep herd that had been grazing just outside the western boundary of the *Caribou Wilderness* protected area, where this pack of wolves that he had been following resided. Isaiah knew that the wolves didn't abide by the boundaries of the park. If the deer population around the park had been higher they would never attack livestock. It was only as a last resort that they did.

Isaiah had a pretty good relationship with the ranchers at this particular sheep ranch. There was a fund that the *Friends of Wolves Society* that Hootman had originated had put aside for just these kinds of emergencies. Being a friend of Hootman and a friend of the *Friends,* enabled Isaiah to draw on these funds. He called Josh Jacobs who was the foreman at the ranch and offered to compensate him for his loss. Josh told Isaiah that all of their sheep were counted for.

"I guess that is why you sleep so well," Isaiah joked. "Then it must be from the new ranch on our southern border. I have not interacted with them before, but I guess I will have to now."

"That's funny," Josh responded to Isaiah's sheep joke, though he had heard it before. "I have not met them yet either, or I could put a good word in for you, as they just moved into this new grazing area fairly recently. Take care Isaiah."

Isaiah got back in his truck and headed south to speak with the new sheep ranchers. It took a while to drive, as he actually had to drive west first, as there was no direct road to get there. The way the crows fly or the wolves' walk was not available to his truck.

Isaiah walked into the ranch office, which was a one story modern glass and redwood building. There was an attractive tall, svelte, red headed woman in fitted workout clothes at a desk in one of the rooms in the front of the building. Her name tag read Stephanie. Isaiah introduced himself and asked to be directed to the foreman of the ranch. Stephanie flirted with him, saying he looked like a wolf in sheep's clothing or something to that effect. She told him that it was a cooperative and that there was no real foreman, and that he could address his concerns to her, and joked that she wouldn't pull the wool over his eyes.

He admitted what he had found in some of the wolf scat that he had submitted the previous week.

"Wow, you are pleading guilty before even being charged, I'm impressed, the last honest man. Yes, we lost a sickly lamb recently, but it really wasn't in any shape to ever be productive for us in our wool shearing operation. There is no way you could have known that from the DNA, I don't think, but I really appreciate that you showed up here in person. Now we know whom I can call if there ever is a bigger problem to our herd. You can leave me your phone and contact information and I can give you mine," Stephanie winked.

"I noticed that most of your sheep seem to look quite healthy with full coats on, so my wolves are assisting you in quality control then? Wolves really have gotten the bad rap, bad PR, for thousands of years probably. I'd like to get the agent for squirrel PR for my wolves," Isaiah flirted back.

"That's funny, you know who also has great PR? God does," Stephanie responded, following up on Isaiah's response to her. "There is a country diner in town, only 20 minutes away, and I'd be honored to take you out for a meal. It's the least that I can do for so truthful a person as you Isaiah."

Again Isaiah felt guilt thinking about Phoebe and being with another pretty young female, but he was really hungry. Being that the restaurant was a few miles past where the ranch was, and he would have to come back that way anyway, he left his truck at the ranch, and went in Stephanie's *Subaru Outback*. On the way out she showed him the shearing building, and the chemical treatment facility. She pointed out the grazing area and he could see numerous sheep hanging out. He noticed again that this woman was picking up on those juices that Nora mentioned, and was turning him on again with her presence, but did not betray herself with any direct words that she said so far. He liked the feelings, but again felt guilty for having those feelings.

"We have 100% *Delaine Merino* sheep at our ranch," Stephanie said and continued. "They are smoother and have less wrinkles and more skin folds so they produce an abundance of fine wool. We do not use any of our sheep for eating. They are only used for their wool."

"As I said, your sheep seem healthy and quite content. It must be about time to sheer the fleece, it seems to me," Isaiah remarked.

"That's right, being that it is almost spring, we will start shearing them in the next couple of weeks. This way they get to stay warm for the winter months and cooler for the summer heat, but also will have some hair or fleece on them to prevent summer sunburns."

"That coincides with the time of year that wolf pups are born, although the two thoughts have little else in common, except that everything reminds me about wolves. I bet your sheep are happy that they don't have to wear those warm coats in the hot California summers," Isaiah responded.

"I think that you would win your bet. Our sheep are some of the happiest sheep in the world, even though we haven't been here that long yet, only setting up this past year. We also will be using sustainable grazing techniques so that we don't destroy the hand that feeds us. They will live a good life out here, and *Merino* sheep will produce wool for a dozen years or more. Do you know why *Merino* wool doesn't itch as much as regular wool?" Stephanie asked.

"I don't know. Perhaps the wool is smoother," Isaiah responded.

"That's true, but it is smoother or doesn't itch because the diameter of the hairs are less, so they bend instead of forcing themselves up against one's skin. Not all *Merino* hair or fleece is the same diameter, so we have special equipment using laser technology to separate the width of the different fleece, and that way we know which will be the least itchy."

They arrived shortly at the diner. The host and hostess were friendly with Stephanie and seated them in a romantic nook by a side window overlooking a pretty wooded area.

"I'm a vegan, like my sheep," Stephanie related. "I don't mind if you want some meat, being a wolf person yourself," she kidded.

"I used to be a vegan, but lately I've been eating meat again. I think I will take the bison burger. It says that they are made from a local ranch, so they must be very fresh indeed," Isaiah said, feeling doubly guilty.

"I've never eaten them here, but my friends have, and they do smell delicious," Stephanie disclosed. "How much time do you spend in the forest with the wolves?" she asked.

"Most of the time I can be found somewhere in the park. I have a small cabin that I usually sleep and cook in, but I also spend nights out in a sleeping bag in a tent, or even under the sky when I'm tracking," Isaiah responded.

"I guess that doesn't leave you much time for a relationship? I'm supposing no wife or kids to worry about?" Stephanie stated in a friendly, yet interrogating manner.

"Funny that you ask me that now. Last week I was single and hadn't had a real relationship since I started working here and well before that. This last weekend, actually only a day or two ago, I went down to Marin for my mom's birthday, and I happened to meet a young lady there, who I fell head over heels over, the first time in my life. I even started fantasizing about having a family with her. That is totally unlike the guy you would have met 3 days ago," Isaiah revealed.

"Ha, that is quite the story. She must be very special for you to change your pattern and conditioning so quickly. So how are you going to arrange to include her in your life?" Stephanie asked.

"That is the question. I don't have an answer to it yet, but I will do anything to have Phoebe, that's her name, close to me. She is not really working now, so I'm hoping that she can join me here for at least a while, and then maybe we can work something out together. I really love my job here, and don't know what I will do if she doesn't want to live with me."

"That is a potential conundrum. I'd love to meet Phoebe when and if she gets here. Having friends around can make a difference. I loved your honesty from when we first met this afternoon, and anyone that you hold in such high repute must also be a remarkable person. I actually had the intention of hitting on you myself, but now that I know the circumstances, I suppose I will have to pass," Stephanie winked.

"Thank you, I appreciate that. That also is funny. You are the second, actually the third beautiful woman that I met today and yesterday who wanted to hit on me. This never happens to me. This woman at the local office who desired me said it was Phoebe's juice on me that makes me attractive to other women. She compared me to a restaurant where no one is eating, as opposed to one that is full of happy customers. That makes as much sense as anything else," Isaiah remarked.

"Well, you are a good looking and an enthusiastic young man. That should count for some points as well. I like that analogy though. I was just in a long relationship, but my fiancé was sneaking on me with someone from the buffalo ranch. It would have been bad enough if he cheated with another of the girls at our ranch, but to do it with a buffalo girl. That was too much for me," Stephanie partly joked.

Just then, Isaiah's phone rang. It was Phoebe. He excused himself and went just outside the diner to speak with her.

"Hi Isaiah, I wanted to check in with you and see how you are doing or being, as I like to say?" Phoebe asked.

"Great, I was having dinner with this person from the sheep ranch on our southern border. It seems some of our wolves helped themselves to a sheep, but as it turns out it was a sickly one, and the ranchers aren't upset at all, actually thankful to the wolves for culling their herd. This person I'm with happens to be an attractive redhead. I thought I should tell you that. I told her about you and she had some designs on me, but backed off after I told her," Isaiah reported, sheepishly.

"Oh, maybe you should go back and finish your dinner. I don't want to prevent you from having fun. It's not like we agreed not to see anyone else. I want you to have as much fun as you can," Phoebe repeated, a bit disconcerted.

"That is true, but this is the second pretty woman that has hit on me today, and I was brought up to only be with one woman at a time, though I admit that I haven't even done much of that. I did feel a bit guilty, but I trust myself to do the right thing," Isaiah responded.

"Okay, no need to feel guilty, after all you are a red blooded young man. I've got a test for you then," Phoebe said, changing her attitude to one of being more open and pleasure oriented. "I think you can take this redhead to bed and do whatever feels good, except no fucking and no kissing. Make her the offer and tell her that I agreed or even desire this. See how she responds. If you feel turned on then go with her, if not, or if she declines for whatever reason, that will be fine too. I want you to have fun,"

Phoebe said again, but this time meaning it. "One more thing, if you do go to bed with this redhead, then I want you to tell me what you did with her, okay? And you can tell me about this other woman who hit on you earlier, when we speak tomorrow."

"Wow, let me think about this for a second. It sounds good I mean, but you are more important to me than anything, and I will only do this if you really want me to, and you are not just saying it," Isaiah answered, sort of.

"I really do. It is your choice of course. I am enjoying this female power over you, and want to use it for your benefit too. So call me tomorrow with a full report," Phoebe said, saying good bye, I love you dearly, and hanging up.

Isaiah went to the bathroom before going back to the table. He wasn't sure what he was going to do yet, and wanted to talk to his reflection in the bathroom mirror and wash his face first. Luckily no one else was in the bathroom. He liked the way he looked. He seemed more confident and he had a gleam in his eye that he hadn't noticed before. "Well, my friend," he said to his own image, "I guess we are going to go for it, right?" He answered himself, "As long as it feels right, and fun, then full steam ahead. Speak your truth and damn the torpedoes," he laughed, and went back to the table.

Isaiah sat back down. Stephanie looked at him intently and said, "So that must have been your girlfriend, Phoebe, right?"

"That's correct," Isaiah answered. Almost getting cold feet again, he decided to speak the truth. "I told her that I met this beautiful redhead at the sheep farm who was taking me out for some good food, and she was jealous at first, then something changed in her, and she challenged me to go have a sexual escapade with you."

"Ha," Stephanie exclaimed, fully blushing. "She certainly is something else, evolved and very generous. I don't know if I'd let my boyfriend, if I had one that is, have a fling with someone, but I'd prefer that to having him cheating on me. Well, I'm more than game, quite horny to tell you the truth. Maybe we should only eat a few bites now, and finish the rest after our liaison. We can go back to my room at the ranch," Stephanie said flirtatiously, and sending certain pheromonic signals to Isaiah.

Isaiah could feel his genitals stirring and starting to become much more interested. "Oh there were a couple of caveats. Phoebe said no fucking and no kissing, and I had to report a full description to her about our dalliance afterwards."

"No problem, I can live with that. I figure there are a couple of activities that we can figure out that we still can do, you think? Do you have any suggestions Mister?" Stephanie responded seductively.

"I must admit that I have not had any sexual dalliance, as you call it, in a long time. Maybe I could give you a massage first, and work my way to your pussy, and then use my hands and mouth to bring you to an orgasm," Isaiah said, still feeling his genitals stirring.

"Oh you are so kind, Isaiah. I could go for that. Then I'd want to ravish you too, running my hands all over your body, including some magic mojo on your dick, till you couldn't take it any longer, then making you beg me to finish you off. I will peak you, over and over, till you are totally responding to my pussy power over you."

Isaiah was getting real hard listening to Stephanie's discourse about ravishing his body and penis relentlessly.

"What will you do if I get on top of you at that point and fuck you when you have surrendered your whole body to me?" Stephanie asked.

Isaiah was feeling so turned on at this time, he didn't know how to answer her, but he tried. "I promised Phoebe, and I want you to promise me that you will honor her wishes too, even though mentally right now I feel kind of like I already inwardly betrayed her."

"I was just playing with you Isaiah. I hope you don't mind. I won't fuck you, unless you beg me to, that is, and even then I may just sit on your face and hump your mouth," Stephanie continued with her verbal sexual assault.

They finished up dinner very quickly after that. Isaiah ate all his fries, as they don't taste very good cold, but the burger that he managed to only take two bites of, he took to go.

They returned to the ranch and went inside the residence complex. There were a couple of Stephanie's coworkers milling about. The kitchen and dining area were communal, as well as a game room and entertaining area. They were all friendly and kidded her about hanging out with a wolf man, after she introduced Isaiah. Stephanie's room was quite small, but she had a large comfy bed and a good sized flat screened TV on the wall. There was a small bathroom with a shower attached to it. Isaiah liked her accommodations, and thought that he could live in a place like this quite comfortably.

Stephanie said, "Let's do finger kissing." She showed Isaiah what she meant, and added, "I think that would be legal under our current agreement."

They each put a finger to the other person's lips and moved them around, using the tip of the fingers and even the back of a finger to provide whatever felt best at the moment, in an almost sort of kissing manner. Stephanie put his finger in her mouth and was sucking on it, almost as if it was a penis, wrapping her tongue around it, and using her mouth as if it was a vagina. This felt way better than Isaiah was expecting. Stephanie then pulled him close to her and still fully clothed, rubbed her body against his. "I can feel that you are still interested," she said, as she gently and slowly moved her palm against his engorged penis.

"That feels really good," Isaiah vocalized after a few strokes. He was slowly and gently following Stephanie's lead, leaving her lips, and now rubbing her breasts through her smooth tight clothing. "Your nipples are quite engorged also," Isaiah remarked.

"Yes, they are very sensitive. You have a nice gentle touch," Stephanie responded, breathing quite heavily. She somehow adjusted his engorged member so that it was lying upward and the most sensitive underneath side was facing her, although his clothes were still on. Stephanie put her palm against his hard penis and pushed it against his lower abdomen, tenderly but assuredly. After pressing and releasing the weight of her hand numerous times, she started rubbing some more in a side to side motion.

"That feels so ggggood," Isaiah moaned on and on. He also did not want to squirt prematurely without even getting his pants off, and knew he couldn't take much more of this at the moment without doing so. He was very horny too, from the turned-on time spent with Phoebe. Semi reluctantly, he pushed her hand aside, and pressed his own right hand against Stephanie's crotch. He could feel her vulva contracting under his hand. He pressed and released as she had done to him.

Stephanie was groaning with pleasure. "You have strong yet gentle hands Isaiah. It really feels sensational. Let's take our clothes off now, and repeat that very provocative scenario."

They removed their clothes rather quickly, although Isaiah had somewhat of a difficult time getting his pants off, with his penis still so engorged. Fully naked, his member was pointing straight at her body. She put her cool hand gently around it and just held it, feeling the throbbing. Isaiah put his right index finger against her facial lips again, and circled it around, pressing in when it felt she was enjoying a specific spot. He put his left middle finger against her crotch and could feel the warm and wetness of her pussy, as she tenderly yet firmly pulled his penis and therefore the rest of him even closer against her.

"Your hand feels amazing around me. My penis feels so engorged. I like the coolness encircling it, as my penis is really hot," Isaiah remarked between moans.

"I think we can skip the massage part," Stephanie said, as she led him to the bed still holding onto his penis. "You can go straight to my pussy now. I really feel like you getting on top of me and kissing and fucking me, but I will just fantasize about that," Stephanie whispered in his ear.

Isaiah feeling more in control and more confident, said, "Get on the bed, lie on your back, and spread your legs. I will do as I see fit and will get to your pussy when I'm ready to."

Stephanie did what she was told, letting go of his throbbing member. Isaiah lay down next to her, but had his head facing in the opposite direction and was lying on his left side. "You have such beautiful red hair covering your pussy. I have never seen such bright red hair down there before. I guess it matches your hair, but it still is surprising. Your pussy is extremely enticing, but I will get there when I see fit."

First he put his hand on her abdomen and pressed firmly. He could feel the contractions starting up again. He lightly massaged her lower abdomen approaching closer to her pussy, then moved his hand to her thigh. "Your thighs are super sexy, super silky, and are super fun to touch," Isaiah said, as he stroked them one at a time in a circular motion, getting closer to her pussy with each cycle.

Stephanie was moaning quite loudly, and when Isaiah finally put his hand on her pussy he could see and feel an abundance of wetness coming from her vagina, and told her that. He started stroking up and down her labia after moving the luscious red pubic hair to either side.

"Your hands feel so amazingly great Isaiah. I'd love it if you pulled back my clitoral hood and rubbed directly on it with some of this lubricant," Stephanie said, as she handed him a tube.

Isaiah took the tube, placed his forearm on her abdomen and pulled back the hood with the base of his palm. He had never really pulled back on a woman's hood before, but it retracted quite effortlessly and he was able to see the naked exposed clitoris with ease. He had applied the lubricant to the tip of his middle finger and placed it directly on the shiny pearl object. As soon as he made contact, Stephanie began moaning and contracting with more vigor. She was quite still, except for the contractions that she was involuntarily having.

After a few strokes, her clitoris engorged to about twice its size and was very much exposed to his view. She had a clear, perhaps slightly whitish ejaculate ooze from her vagina. He told her what he saw and Stephanie moaned her approval, and told him that it felt so good, and to keep doing whatever he was doing. Isaiah no longer had to pull back on her hood, and kept giving her a soft rhythmic stroke directly on her clitoris.

After a number of minutes of being in this blissful orgasmic state, Stephanie put her hand around his penis again. Her hand wasn't as cold as before, but still felt fantastic to Isaiah. He continued to gently stroke on her clitoris, as she held his engorged member in her hand, pressing softly but assuredly, and slowly moving it in little circles. Isaiah told her how good her hand felt. Isaiah was producing even more exquisite responses from Stephanie's pussy, stroking her clitoris and peaking her by taking little side trips to her labia, and then back home to stroking her clitoris. His consistent exquisite stroking and teasing brought Stephanie significantly higher and higher.

Stephanie said, "This is amazing, better than I expected. I love how you control my orgasm by just stopping before I am ready to stop, and then surprising me with more. You have a great cock too, Isaiah. Let's take a little break. I am going to turn on my side now and play with your erotic zones some more. You can lie on your back now if you like, relax, and perhaps still stroke my clitoris some as I stroke you."

She still had his penis in her hand as she turned on her side. He knew that he could not resist her any longer and did what she asked. She put some cool lubricant on his still engorged penis with her other hand and started stroking it. She had him real good and had him in her sexual power again. He was real hard, and he admitted his vulnerability to her, though she was still getting off at the same time, and it felt like she was almost doing him with her contracting pussy.

The energy cycled from her awareness to his awareness and back and forth it traveled, as they were almost becoming one buzzing turned on body of excited neurons. They took turns putting the focus of their attention on his nervous system, until Isaiah was about to ejaculate, and then back to hers, which allowed him to come back down from that height. Each time that he came back down, she would know when that was, and start bringing him higher again, using one specific type of stroke at a time, but varying what kind of stroke with each peak. She stroked his penis with both hands, a full-length stroke from the base of his cock, and even underneath his scrotum where his engorged hidden cock was, and up to the corona and head of his penis, and then back down. On another peak she lightly stroked the underneath area of his penis up and down with just one finger. She pulled on his testicles at times to show him how much she owned him sexually.

Isaiah had never felt this much sexual ecstasy in his life, until Stephanie upped the anti when she placed her mouth against the tip of his engorged penis and licked the head of his penis as she continued to stroke the shaft. She could only do this for a few strokes, as she sensed that he was about to explode, and had to back off for a few moments, and then start up again.

She took her mouth off for a few seconds and told him that he tasted delicious. She put it back on and brought him into a super intense state. Over and over she played with him like that, while still in continual orgasm herself, as he stroked her pussy with confidence.

Isaiah was moaning really loud in total bliss, and Stephanie teased him mercilessly a couple of more times, almost bringing him to ejaculation on each occasion, and finally allowing him to explode into her mouth with a full load of sweet ejaculate, as she gently coaxed with her gentle hand and purposeful tongue, every drop of it out of his slowly softening penis.

Stephanie moved to lie in the same direction as Isaiah so that she was now spooning his body from behind. She put his top leg between her legs and humped his thigh with her vulva to bring her own body back down to a reasonable level of excitement.

"Ha, that was more fun than I can remember. I must have gained at least a pound from swallowing your delicious ejaculate. I think that I will definitely remember this to my dying day," Stephanie whispered in his ear.

"Ha or wow for me likewise." Isaiah continued, "I am overwhelmed. I never experienced being peaked in that way, and so many times, and getting so high as you just took me. Now I'm wondering what Phoebe will be thinking when I tell her how much fun I had. I hope she doesn't get upset. I learned so much from this experience, so I imagine that she will be the beneficiary of it too."

"She is a lucky woman. You are an amazing man. You have great hands and a great cock. You are kind, communicative, and she better appreciate you. I still would love to meet her someday, if she is up to it, and if for some reason your relationship doesn't work out, you know where to find me."

Chapter 12
Phoebe Isaiah

Leaving the ranch, Isaiah felt exhaustively fantastic. After saying good-bye and giving Stephanie a big full body hug, still no kissing, he got in his truck and headed back to his cabin. First he ate the rest of his bison burger, and it even tasted way better than it had earlier.

Being the kind of guy that Isaiah was, he wanted to tell Phoebe the truth, as he had promised her. He would tell her all that occurred and not skip over any erotic parts even if it meant that she might get jealous or whatever, as long as she still wanted to hear the details that is. He decided to call Phoebe almost right away before he forgot any of the many specifics.

After saying their affable hellos, Isaiah immediately said, "I wanted to call you right away Phoebe. I just finished my date with Stephanie, and I had a fantastic time, better than I expected. I want to thank you for making it possible, and wanted to report what happened, like you asked, before I forgot any of the specifics."

"You better tell me," Phoebe half joked. "I've been running all kinds of scenarios in my head, so how did you start?"

"We went to her dormitory. It is almost a commune with residents having small private rooms. She has a cute bedroom with a large bed, and a nice bathroom. There is a communal kitchen and a number of other public areas nearby, but we closed the door, and we were all by ourselves. She put on some light opera music, which I usually don't care for, but these were all beautiful female soprano voices, and the sounds seemed all quite sexy."

"That's all fine, but get to the nitty gritty, Isaiah," Phoebe remarked impatiently.

Isaiah started again, "Stephanie suggested that we put our fingers on each other's lips in lieu of kissing. It felt like we were breaking a taboo, but staying in the limits of what you requested. It felt like she was almost touching my penis the way she slowly engaged my lips. We were both getting more and more turned on," Isaiah related and continued.

"Stephanie then pulled me against her body in a full body hug. She was rubbing her body up against me, and I was getting quite turned on. She was wearing an athletic tight outfit, very sexy. She used her hand to gently touch my you know what through my clothes, and it felt sensational. She kind of just held it there and felt my throbbing. I rubbed her nipples gently too, and they were responding, and became really firm under her shirt. We were both getting more and more turned on. She somehow shifted my penis thru my pants, having it lay against my belly with the underneath side of the shaft facing towards her. She pressed her palm, I think, against my shaft, and repeated pushing it toward my belly, and then releasing the pressure. It was really great. She then began, starting slowly, moving her palm around, and I was getting so high, moaning loudly to her movements that I was almost ready to squirt already, so I pushed her hand aside semi reluctantly, and pressed my hand against her vulva in a similar stroke that she had just done to me. Her pussy was very heated. I could tell she was wet, and contracting already. She was also moaning quite loudly."

"Hold on a second Isaiah. This is really getting me hot, and I'm getting very turned on listening. I've been rubbing myself through my clothing while you talked. I'm going to get some lubrication and pleasure myself while you tell me the rest, okay?" Phoebe said, as she took the phone to the bedroom and pulled her jeans off, and got on top of the bed. She found her pussy to be very wet, and she started stroking herself. "All right Isaiah, you can continue now."

"Let's see where were we? Oh yare, we were both moaning, and Stephanie suggested that we both get naked, and continue without our clothes. My penis was very engorged, and I had a hard time (pun intended) removing my pants and underpants. When undressed, it was pointing directly at her. She got undressed quickly and was up against me again, real fast. She gently seized my penis, just held it there with her grip and feeling it fully in her own body, she reported, and also reported how it was throbbing in her hand. I put my hand or middle finger actually, against her vulva and felt the warmth and wetness and gentle contractions of her pussy. She told me again that I had a really nice touch. She then circled my penis and pulled me closer to her, using it as if it were a handle. We were both moaning, and then I told her something similar to how her cool hands felt so great encircling my hot penis. She used her other hand to squeeze my butt cheeks and I did the same to hers."

"That's so erotic," Phoebe interrupted. "I'm rubbing my pussy now too, and it is wet, and turned on, and also contracting. I also just squeezed my own butt cheeks, and it feels as if you are doing it to me, Isaiah. Okay you can continue now."

"I'm starting to feel more again, but it's your pussy I'm imagining Phoebe," Isaiah responded, and continued his narrative. "Stephanie still holding my cock, led me to her bed as if I was her sex slave. I enjoyed that role, but thought maybe she wanted me to take more control, so I told her to lie down on her back and spread her legs. That worked. She obeyed and told me that I could go straight to her pussy with my hands. I decided to take more control. I told her that I would get there when I was ready to, and started teasing her by playing with her lower abdomen first, using light provocative strokes, getting close to her genitals, and then doing the same to her thighs. I must admit, her thighs are strong and smooth, and quite sexy. She also has bright red pubic hair, matching her head, which surprised me for some reason. She kidded me and said something about fantasizing about me getting on top of her, and kissing and fucking her. Her thighs felt really pleasurable to touch too. She was moaning even louder now, as I put my hand finally on her pussy labia. She was very wet but still handed me some lubricant, and asked if I could pull back her clitoral hood, and stroke her clitoris with it. None of the girls or women that I've slept with ever requested that, and I was surprised how good it felt to my finger, and her keen response."

Phoebe was following Isaiah's story and stroking herself in the areas that he described. She was feeling lots of pleasurable sensations, and was truly enjoying the description.

"I just pulled back my own hood and put some lubricant on my clitoris, and it feels fantastic. I'm glad she informed you about that. I'm benefitting from your date already, and I plan to educate you even further. You will become quite the clitoral scholar, clitorate, as I heard it mentioned," Phoebe said, interrupting Isaiah, but then requested that he continue.

"I look forward to that," Isaiah responded, and renewed his account. "After only a few strokes directly on the upper left side of her clitoris it engorged to about twice its size, and became very much exposed. She had a clear, perhaps whitish ejaculate ooze from her vagina, and she was moaning loudly. She told me how good it felt and to keep doing what I was doing. I no longer had to pull back on her hood, and kept giving her a soft rhythmic stroke directly on her clitoris with the tip of my middle finger."

Isaiah could hear Phoebe making ecstatic sounds from her end of the phone call. Luckily there were no other cars on the road.

"After a number of minutes of being in this blissful orgasmic state, Stephanie put her hand around my penis again. It felt exciting and very sensational as she first just held it there, as I continued stroking her clitoris. She then started gently squeezing it with her whole hand, pressing softly but assuredly, and slowly moving it in little circles. I told her how amazing her hand felt. I kept on bringing her up and then down a bit, to peak her back up again, numerous times. She told me that I had great hands and a great cock, and that she loved the way my cock felt in her hand and then asked for a short break. She turned on her left side, and said that I could lie on my back. She asked me to continue stroking her clitoris gently while she applied and slid some cool lubricant to my hot engorged penis, moving some of my pubic hairs aside. Her clitoris was really engorged and easy to manipulate without having to look at it now. She was then using both of her hands to stimulate me. It felt like she was doing me with the repeated contractions of her pussy, which kept on happening. I was in a total sensation mode, and she had me in her pussy powered control."

Phoebe was stroking herself to Isaiah's reenactment, and feeling tremendous amounts of sensation too. "I can feel your hands on my pussy. And I can feel your cock in my hands," she commented, squealing with delight as if she was Stephanie, giving Isaiah the green light to continue.

"The energy was traveling thru us like a cyclotron, and at times I didn't know what part of it was me and what part of it was her. She peaked me numerous times by changing the stroke from long full hand strokes to just one finger lightly on the underneath part of my penis. Then she raised the stakes and sweetened the pot; put her lips on the tip of my penis and continued to stroke with her two hands. I could hardly take this much pleasure and she knew it, and backed off in the nick of time. I thought I would explode with ejaculation a number of times, but she knew when to stop and peak me. I had never felt this much sexual ecstasy in my life. I was in total bliss. Over and over she took me to the edge and finally allowed me to explode a tremendous amount of semen into her mouth, as she slowed down her strokes and gently enticed the last drops of semen from it with her tongue."

Phoebe was loudly moaning along with the recounting of Isaiah's sexcapade. "Wow, you just gave me a great orgasm too, Isaiah. I can't believe how much fun I just had in this seemingly vicarious position. I was jealous thinking about you and her, but that did not stop me from having a great orgasm. I no longer feel excluded, as I now feel totally included. I believe that I am going to come up to see you next weekend for sure now, so you better replenish your semen supply, as I know that I will want some first hand. I have some tricks of my own that will take you places you have not even dreamed of," Phoebe teased, turning on Isaiah again from many miles away.

"I am relieved that you are not upset, and happy that you have been so generous with me. I may just reward you as well with some of my own tricks, as you say. This went way better than I thought, in so many ways, so really thank you Phoebe for creating the opportunity. I am now heading into a zone where cell phone reception is poor, so we may get disconnected soon. I will call you tomorrow," Isaiah said, as the connection broke up on cue.

Phoebe fell asleep from her orgasmic climb, and woke up a few hours later to change into her pajamas and quickly fall back to sleep. The next morning she woke up refreshed. She decided to call Stephanie.

Being an investigative reporter it was simple for Phoebe to get Stephanie's phone number. "Hi Stephanie, I'm Phoebe, Isaiah's friend."

Stephanie had the thought that Phoebe might be upset, but just responded, "Hi Phoebe, thank you for being so generous with your boyfriend."

"You are very welcome. I wanted you to know that Isaiah called me last night and reported the great time he had with you yesterday in full detailed account. I am not mad at you if that was what you were thinking. I am grateful and had a great orgasm while I was listening to his rendition of the event. I must admit I was jealous thinking about the two of you together, but I wanted to let you know that I feel perfectly okay with it now."

"Oh good, I am glad, actually relieved, to hear you say that. I had so much fun with him. You certainly have a good guy there. I only went ahead with it after you gave your blessings, but I still felt a bit guilty for doing so. Basically, I think us women should stick together, and not go poaching into other women's territory. I told Isaiah, and now I will tell you. I would love to meet you, if you ever come up this way to visit or to live. I know he wants that, but he wasn't sure about your moving to the wilderness. Isaiah mentioned that you used to be on television, and I got to admit that you were one of the hottest reporters that I looked forward to watching, so I feel I kind of know you already."

"Thanks Stephanie. Those days seem so long ago. I think I may move up your way eventually or sooner perhaps, but as you may know we only just met a couple of days ago. I found myself feeling so comfortable and turned on around him, if that is possible, which obviously it must be. I am coming up there, and will be visiting him this weekend, and make sure it wasn't just a dream that we both had. I don't mind wherever I live, if it feels right. I am a journalist as you know, and can have a home base anywhere I choose. Perhaps it would be easier to do that in London, or New York City, or LA, but with modern communications and deliveries, I don't think where really matters that much anymore. I'm attracted with where my life situation has taken me, to being in more natural settings, so you may be seeing me sooner than you think," Phoebe said, sipping a cup of coffee to keep her throat moist from talking.

"Being out in the sticks definitely has its benefits as well as its drawbacks. You won't find a Starbucks on every corner, but you will find a more relaxed and pleasurable way to live, I think. Isaiah is real, not a dream, though he is dreamy, and he is also ready to be chosen by you. He confided to me that he was already thinking of raising a family with you, so if that is what you want, and I really hope that you do, then it will all work out." Stephanie continued, "Let's stay in touch, as I said, I really would love to meet you, and talking with you has been fun and informative."

"Isaiah also mentioned how attractive you are, yet you seem so down to earth and friendly. Even though people have me as beautiful, I consider it better to enjoy life when I'm putting attention out there and not on me and how I look. It did not come naturally however, I had to work on that. I think many beautiful women have a hard time being happy, and are often depressed. Fine-looking women are noticing what is wrong or out of place on themselves, while less beautiful women can appreciate the parts and places where they are beautiful. I think we may be sisters in that respect, and look forward to meeting you too, Stephanie. Bye for now," Phoebe said, as they both hung up their phones.

Chapter 13
Phoebe Isaiah

More than anything, Phoebe wanted to be with and to see Isaiah. She arranged her life so that she was able to drive up north to be with Isaiah the next Friday. They were both looking forward to being together again. They had texted and spoken at least once a day that week.

Phoebe arrived while it was still light out. She had no trouble finding his cabin thanks to modern GPS, though it was quite isolated in the woods. Isaiah was there to greet her. The last time he had seen Phoebe was when her sister in law or rather her ex sister in law had shown up to break up their little party.

Phoebe was hungry, tired, and her neck ached from sitting in the car for a good part of the day. She wanted to show her best side off to Isaiah, but crankiness trumped sexiness when she first arrived. He gave her a big hug, as she got out of her car. He could feel the tenseness in her body and wanted her to relax and feel better. Both of their unwarranted expectations that they would just miraculously glide into bed and have pleasure all weekend were quickly dashed.

"I can't believe I have you in my arms again my darling," Isaiah stated. "You weren't just a dream after all. You must be tired and hungry from the long drive. How about a hot shower, and I'll fix you something to eat? Maybe a neck and back massage too. I can feel how tense your body feels."

"Oh Isaiah, you are as kind as I remember. I guess it is kind of obvious that I feel a bit crimped. I had plans to knock your socks off after arriving, but I think your offer of a hot shower, some food, and a massage are what the doctor ordered," Phoebe said gratefully.

They went inside his cabin. It was more spacious from the inside than it seemed from without. It was kind of like a very large studio apartment, with a bathroom off to the side. There was a dining and kitchen area on one side of the room with a genuine Wolf Range for cooking. Phoebe wondered how he afforded that, because she knew they were expensive. There was a large fireplace against the back wall. The king sized bed was on the far side of the room from the kitchen area, near the bathroom. The whole cabin had a nice odor to it, almost like a bakery.

Isaiah gave Phoebe a towel. "I have one of those tankless water heaters, so after less than a minute you should have all the hot water that you desire. You can take as long a shower as you like."

"Thanks, this is perfect. I thought we might have to boil the water over a fire. I usually don't like taking long showers, with California being in a drought situation all the time, but I may just indulge myself today," Phoebe responded, feeling somewhat less tense already, and impressed that the cabin was hooked up to both electricity and gas.

"I've got well water here, and it supposedly is quite full, so don't feel guilty. The only problem is that I don't have a blow dryer," Isaiah informed her.

"That's okay, I brought one with me. A girl scout must be prepared," Phoebe joked.

While Phoebe was showering, Isaiah went to the kitchen and put together his favorite tuna fish recipe. He mixed it up with sesame oil, ginger, pistachios, a dash of cayenne pepper, and a spoon of organic avocado oil mayonnaise, and canned sliced water chestnuts. He sliced some fresh sourdough bread he had baked in the morning, and added a wedge of Butter Lettuce and homemade coleslaw to the plate.

"Wow again, I'm impressed. This food looks delicious. I am really hungry. Now I know what smelled so good when I walked in. It was the sourdough bread you must have baked earlier. The shower really hit the spot. You have great water pressure and plenty of hot water. I feel way more relaxed already. I can't wait to taste your concoction here, Isaiah."

They sat down and Phoebe did not waste time by saying grace or giving thanks, but dove into the food, or actually, she had the food dive into her mouth. She made yum sounds but did not waste time on speaking words. After finishing the sandwich and starting on a second one, she finally said, "This is the best tuna fish that I ever ate. The bread is so fresh and tasty and the slaw is heavenly. What did you add to the tuna that makes it taste so great? No, don't tell me. Let me guess. I taste some toasted sesame oil, some cayenne, and some grated ginger. I love the toasted pistachios and a hint of mayo too."

"You pretty much nailed it. It's my mother's recipe. She also gave me her secret recipe for the coleslaw, so I can't divulge what goes into that," Isaiah responded, with a pleased look in his eyes. "I was going to take you out to town for dinner, but it's too far, and you were too famished, and besides, I like this food better anyway, so thanks for being so hungry."

"It's nice to know that you can create tasty dishes quickly. I was planning to seduce you upon arriving, but with the long drive and my hunger, and now I'm really full. You should have stopped me from eating so much," Phoebe stated after finishing her second sandwich and the rest of her slaw.

"I've learned not to get in the way of women and their food. I remember how you ate that omelet in Olema, as if you were a voracious wolf," Isaiah kidded. "I was not going to interrupt. I've waited my whole life for you, so I can wait a little more."

"Would you like that massage now or are you too full for that too?" Isaiah asked, not being very hopeful.

"Yup, my belly is too full to lie down now. But maybe you can massage my neck and shoulders in this chair right here," Phoebe answered encouragingly.

"Sure, I'd love to. Let me clear the table and wash my hands first," Isaiah responded cheerfully.

"Ahh, that feels wonderful Isaiah. Stephanie was right. You do have great hands. You are right on the spot there. Yes, you got it. Get that knot. Ahh, that feels so much better already. I think I texted you that I spoke with Stephanie earlier today. I like her, and she seems to like me too. She would love to meet me sometime."

Isaiah began to use his elbow to work out the knots, and he could feel them relinquishing their grip on her trapezius and deltoid muscles. He dug his thumbs into her supraspinatus muscles, and she squealed a bit, but appreciated the removal of pain after he stopped. He massaged the back of her neck, feeling for any tension, and removing it with his thumbs. To finish the massage, Isaiah rubbed Phoebe's upper arms with firm pressure.

"Wow, I really use that word around you a lot, but I feel brand new, like a new born, though I'm not sure how great a newborn really feels. Speaking of which, Stephanie told me that you told her that being with me made you think about having a family for the first time in your life. I'm approaching that age when a woman must decide about having a child, if I am going to have one from this body," Phoebe stated in a matter of fact way, her mind loosened up as well as her body.

"That's direct, and I like that part of you too, and I love the whole package that I feel is you. What I am saying is yes, I would do anything that you want. I trust you, even though we really have not spent a whole lot of time together. I am usually more deliberate, and do not act spontaneously, but you and me feels so right to me, that I whole heartedly support whatever you want to do. I don't make a whole lot of money, which you probably know already, so I think you would be taking the bigger risk than me," Isaiah said, with true love in his eyes.

Phoebe got up from the chair and took Isaiah's head between her hands and slowly but surely began to kiss him in such a passionate way that their lips merged where they could no longer tell the difference between one another, other than they both felt a sensational energy circulating from their lips spreading over their entire tingling bodies and into their loins.

Phoebe finally released his head. They were both breathing deeply, and Phoebe said, "You are perfect for me Isaiah. We don't have to worry about money. I received a big insurance payout from *ABC,* plus I settled with Daniels's private insurance company for another huge sum as a monthly annuity. They didn't want to pay the full amount because there never was a body found, but they finally succumbed to a deal, before it went to court. I also saved a bunch from when I worked, so money is the least of my worries."

Phoebe took Isaiah's hand in hers. "How about we go for a short walk around here before it gets dark, and then I'll show you a couple of things under the sheets."

Isaiah felt his crotch respond to that potential offer, "Yes to both, a walk, and a big yes to being shown a couple of things under the sheets."

He closed the door behind him, but he did not lock it. Phoebe noticed that there was no lock on the door anyway. There was a sort of a yard in the front next to his driveway. In the back of the house was a larger yard though neither was of manicured grass. There were redwoods and other trees scattered around in a haphazard fashion and a small garden area that looked like it wasn't well attended to. There was a small stone deck in back where a couple of outdoor chairs and a metal table rested. At the end of the yard was a small flowing stream. There seemed to be an abundance of birds flitting about at this dusk hour looking for a place to spend the night. The sounds of the birds and the stream filled Phoebe with pleasurable and comforting sensations that had her intensely sense the moment and her own body.

They walked down to the stream, which was flowing rather quickly from the last of the winter rains, and the snow beginning to melt higher up the mountain.

"I really love it here. It is so romantic being here with you. I love this stream. I really get off on the sounds back here. The resonances of the birds chirping and the steady flowing of the water puts me in a state of presence that I don't often feel unless I deliberately meditate back home," Phoebe stated affectionately to Isaiah.

"That's one of the reason that I love it out here. The natural sounds of the earth and the animals that live here are music to my ears as well. Can you hear that distant call of the wolves from over there? They are meeting up first, and then will be going out on their nightly hunt," Isaiah asked, pointing in a north easterly direction.

"Now that you mention it, I do. It's not quite as comforting as the chirping birds, but I think I will change my mind about that quickly, being with such a good friend of theirs," Phoebe responded, after closing her eyes and listening in the direction Isaiah had pointed.

"That loud one that howls first is the alpha male that I call Barack. The second voice is the alpha female Rebecca Lobo, who will be giving birth soon. She is too far into her pregnancy to go out on the hunt tonight, but she is partying with the others before they depart. I will introduce you to them tomorrow," Isaiah explained.

Isaiah pulled Phoebe to him and put his arms around her, as he had done at the beach the week before. He could feel her firm yet still soft in certain places body against his. She was quivering in a sensual response kind of way, and it made him hug her even tighter. She put her arms around his body and they squeezed each other. He inhaled her essence and kissed the side of her neck. She moaned blissfully, and he went to her earlobe, moving her hair aside with one hand, putting his lips around it, taking his time, and then gently tugging on her earlobe with his mouth. Phoebe enjoyed the sensation and listened to his steady breathing right upon her ear, in rhythm with the stream. He put one hand behind her head, feeling her long soft hair and her solid scalp underneath. Looking directly in her eyes from above, he slowly bent his head and moved his mouth toward hers. When he got so close that he could no longer see her eyes, he put his slightly open mouth directly on her more than receptive slightly puckered lips, and began to kiss her gently with all the love that he felt inside.

Phoebe put her attention on her lips and could feel the sensation building stronger, and her yearning for this intimacy accepted with a genuine endorsement. She felt like sparks were created between their lips that sent an electronic signal to her genitals and cycled back to her lips and into Isaiah's body. She could feel his engorgement against her body and enjoyed that power. She welcomed the vibrations of the wolves' beautiful howls echoing throughout her perception.

Isaiah fully enjoyed his engorgement and equated it to the affection he felt from this beautiful spirit that moved his desires. She was moving her sultry body against his turned on body in a most provocative way, responding to his mouth's incursion with her own luring lips and enticing tongue. Her total surrender to his facial parry drew him into her, where he now capitulated to her. Her fragrance so clean, yet so deliciously feminine, intoxicated him into further probes with his own tongue. She trapped him in her mouth where he felt she now held his tongue as her prisoner, even though he was the one who originally believed himself to be the perpetrator. He was more than willing to remain that way for however long she wished. She had the trump card and played it perfectly, taking charge of his body like a virtuoso playing the violin, and they still had all their clothes on. He felt totally connected to this feminine quintessence, and was ready to take her, or be taken to bed at any given time now.

The kiss lasted and lasted, as if they were in some magical osculatory intertwining universe. When they opened their eyes at the exact same moment, the sun had completely set, and the almost full moon was out in full force. Isaiah howled with his best wolf imitation. Phoebe tried to imitate it as well, and for a first effort it was not bad.

She really wanted him now and led him back into the cabin. Isaiah was still engorged, yet had the wherewithal to add a log to the fire, put on some music, and light a thick candle by the bed, which became the only light in the room besides that of the fireplace. Meanwhile, Phoebe had ripped off all her clothing and was totally naked in front of him.

"Wow, see I say wow often too, at least around you. You are even more beautiful naked. I had fantasies of what you looked like undressed, but they don't compare to the real you," Isaiah remarked, as he removed his clothes quickly but carefully, still sporting a large engorged penis pointing directly at her.

They walked towards each other and Isaiah put his right hand between her thighs and slowly moved it up and down, getting closer to her pussy with every iteration. He could feel the warmth and wetness between her legs the closer he got to her pussy. Her hands were not idle either. She used the back of her hand and her arm to gently graze and titillate his engorged member. They both yowled some more, but more in a sexual manner than like your average wolf howl.

"Soon I'm going to rub my strong thighs all over your penis and make you howl some more Isaiah. Then I will get on top of you and insert it into my wet pussy," Phoebe addressed Isaiah and his penis, taking her hand and putting it on his throbbing appendage as she spoke.

"That feels so damn good," Isaiah yelped. He retaliated, and put his hand directly on her wet pussy, dipping his middle finger at her vaginal opening and spreading the wetness to her clitoral pearl. At the same time he put his mouth on her left nipple and gently squeezed it, and then sucking it tenderly between his lips, licking it at the same time, and synchronizing that to the movements of his finger upon her labia and clitoris.

"You got me real real good there. You know how to touch me just right Isaiah. My pussy is yours. My breasts are yours. Do what you want with them," Phoebe moaned, her body already in an orgasmic state.

His stroking and sucking and licking did not stop her from probing his defenses. Phoebe moved her thigh against his penis, which she had manipulated to just the right position. She rubbed his penis with her thigh at the same time that he was pleasuring her. Isaiah felt surrounded by her hand and thigh against his member, and realized that she could take him inside her whenever she wanted.

Isaiah wanted to give her some of her own medicine before she totally overwhelmed him with her sexuality. He lifted her up and carried her to the bed. He spread her legs and lay down between them and lowered his mouth to her pussy. Using his hands to expose her vulva and clitoris from its hood, he explored her pussy with his tongue, as he slowly stroked her labia up and down, again and again, each time going upon her clitoris at the top of the stroke, before retreating back down. Then he isolated his tongue on her fully exposed and bulbous clitoris, licking in a steady short rhythmic motion, while pressing and releasing, over and over again, with his knuckles upon her vaginal opening.

Phoebe was loudly moaning, even howling again, interspersed with words and semi words, saying, "Ah, ah, ah, you got me, you got me ah, ah, so good, ah, ah, paradise, oh my God, Isaiah you are my master," as she continued coming with stronger and stronger contractions spreading from her pussy down her legs and up to the top of her head.

Isaiah lifted his mouth to peak her, and to give his tongue a break, and said, "You taste so delicious Phoebe. Your pussy is as smooth as an abalone shell, and so delectable. You are getting off amazing too. I love you more than anything. I love sucking your pussy."

This short break was all Phoebe needed to turn the game back in her favor, though who's favor was probably not exactly true. She moved her legs together and trapped Isaiah's still elongated and engorged penis between her feet.

"What are you doing?" Isaiah asked, but he already knew the answer. She was taking control back and there was nothing he could do to prevent it, even if he wanted to. She enticed him to get on the bed and then rolled him over on his back. Phoebe put some lubricant on his hot penis, and then placed it between her calf muscles as she slowly moved them erotically against his phallus.

"I'm going to pin your cock under my calf now. There is no escape," Phoebe asserted, with total sexual confidence.

She then pinioned it under her left calf and hardly moved it at all. Then she began to move it faster against his throbbing member, as Isaiah was howling from every cell of his body in corporeal elation, about to spill his seed, when Phoebe masterfully stopped for a few seconds before restarting her sexual offensive.

"I've got you now Mister. You had me real good there, but it's my turn to get you now," Phoebe said, as she moved on top of him. She put her hand upon his penis and gave him a few more delicious strokes, before easily inserting it between her legs into her still very wet and accepting pussy. She rhythmically started to fuck him, both of them howling in delight.

Isaiah was in so much ecstasy, and each time she came down with her thighs and butt upon his body he would gasp with delight. Isaiah whispered, "Oh baby, you are amazing, so sexy, you got me ah, ah, oh wow. I can't take much more of this. I'm going to squirt."

Phoebe could feel his secondary erection growing inside her. She knew to stop moving for a few seconds to peak Isaiah before he squirted. Then she would start again, the peaks coming quicker now, as he was howling without words each time she renewed her sexual conquest.

Phoebe was in a very high orgasmic state herself, feeling his engorgement filling up her vagina way more than she ever had felt before. His body and its appendage were reaching into the depths of her, and even past her body, into her soul. She knew that his enlarged penis was shared by the two of them and that she was riding and being ridden at the same time. She felt one with the universe and howled again and again to broadcast her bliss, and because it felt so good in her throat to do so. As she started her ultimate ride she could feel him getting even bigger and bigger. She rode his explosion like she had never ridden before. His ejaculation came in strong penetrating eruptions, like her personal Mount Vesuvius. Both of them were seeing supernova like explosions in their mind's eyes.

Phoebe stayed in the proverbial saddle until the last of the waves of emissions were over. She slowly dismounted her wild stallion and they held each other in their arms, and allowed their bodies to return to a semblance of normality before they could speak.

After a number of minutes of slowly returning back to the planet in their space capsule; finally opening up the parachute, bringing them safely back to earth.

Isaiah spoke first, "I felt like a rocket ship that was blasting into outer space, with booster rockets being released every time you started moving again. I was in hyper drive and you felt so good surrounding me, and piloting me to places that I have never been. Then the final explosion, and I now know why they call it the *La petit mort* or the little death, as I didn't know if I would ever return to life as I had known it."

"You were so big inside me, Isaiah. You filled every square millimeter of my vagina, and it felt like your soul and mine were combining. The sensation I felt was more than tremendous. I could feel you getting bigger and bigger with each thrust, and my clitoris was so engorged and engaged every time I rode you on the way down. We have a perfect fit that I never had before. It feels like you were built just for me, and I am so happy that you seem to share my desire."

"Phoebe, the way your body fit and controlled my sex by every little and big movement that you made proves to me that your desires are my desires and that your body was created to be a match with mine. I loved how you tasted, so delicious, and how responsive your clitoris was to my tongue and finger. I loved making you howl that one time that I slipped my tongue from your opening to your clitoris, when I told you that you sounded like a true wolf," Isaiah said, as they continued holding on to each other and falling asleep in that position.

Isaiah was the first to wake up. He was spooning Phoebe when he awoke, his arms wrapped around her torso. The room was quite cool, as the fireplace had only some embers glowing, and they had fallen asleep on top of the covers. The candle had totally been used up, but the sun was rising and the light was starting to come through the window facing east. He felt like they fit together like a finished jigsaw puzzle. He didn't want to get up, but he had to pee urgently. He put the covers over Phoebe, and when he peed it was hard to first get the stream flowing, as some residual semen had thickened at the end of his urethra. His urine finally came out, and it splattered around the toilet, before he could direct the stream into the proper direction. He remembered that joke, for your information, the kidneys are for urine formation. He also remembered what a great time they had had, and that it was the first time they had slept together. It seemed like they had been together for an amazingly long and fun stretch of time, not just this short amount of time. Maybe that is what Einstein meant about time being relative.

He put another log on the fire and Phoebe began to stir. "Come back to bed, Isaiah. I want your body against mine again to warm me up."

Isaiah quickly joined Phoebe back in bed, and put the covers over Phoebe and himself, and got back into that spooning position. "The room will warm up now, as I just put a log on," he whispered in her ear, and started kissing her neck and ear lobe again. "I just love your lobes, and I can't get enough of your neck either. Good thing I'm not a vampire."

Phoebe was purring. She also had to pee now, but didn't want to get out of bed either until the room got warmer. "I love your tenderness and warmth," she exclaimed, as the room quickly got warmer. "I have to go reluctantly and pee now, but I will come back, and you can continue where you left off. Maybe some pre-pancakes breakfast hanky-panky, if you are up for it, okay?"

"Are you kidding? My pleasure," he stated.

While she was in the bathroom, her phone rang a number of times. She wondered who would be calling her so early in the morning. She looked at the phone when she got out of the bathroom, and one call was from her mother, and one from her father, and another from Rachel. There was a text from Bella too, wanting her to contact her right away.

"Everyone is calling me so early this morning. This can't be a coincidence, and all these calls worry me. This never happens. I wonder what is going on," Phoebe puzzled.

"You should probably find out then," Isaiah added.

"I will call my dad first, as he is the nicest of the bunch," Phoebe responded.

"Hi dad, what can be so urgent that you are calling me this early in the morning?"

"Hi Phoebe, you must have heard by now, haven't you?" her dad asked.

"Heard what? I'm up north with my new friend Isaiah."

"Oh my, there is some great news. Daniel walked into the American embassy in Islamabad today. He is alive and supposedly okay. It says that he is going to be sent to *Ramstein Airbase* in Germany."

"What? I mean wow. That's great dad," Phoebe asserted, but actually feeling heaviness in her heart. She had loved Daniel, but now she loved Isaiah. Even though it had been only a few days, she felt like he was her soul mate, if there was such a thing. Daniel was the past. He didn't want children and now she did. She didn't want the life in the limelight anymore, and if she went back with Daniel she could well expect that. All these thoughts flashed into her head. She felt guilty for not having happier thoughts on his being alive, but she had finally put his death behind her after all these years, and now he resurrects. It wasn't fair, she thought, and then laughed at herself for paying attention to the voice in her head.

"Thanks dad. Can you do me a favor and call mom and tell her that I spoke with you. I don't really want to speak with her now. I have to process this, and she won't help at all there. I love you, etc., etc." and they hung up after he had agreed to her request.

"Isaiah, I guess you figured out why they were all contacting me. Apparently, Daniel is alive and is on his way to Germany. He will probably be calling me soon too. Who knows what he is like now and what he wants. I don't know what to do. I love you in this short time more than I ever loved him in all those years we were together. He wasn't a bad guy, maybe a little self important of an attitude, but he was, or still is brilliant. I finally started living again, and I don't want to go back to being his wife. I also know that I am with child or embryo, let's call it. I don't know how I know, but I just have that intuition. That was the best fuck of my life last night and I had baby dreams all night," Phoebe said, letting Isaiah know what thoughts were jumping around in her mind; texting back Bella and Rachel at the same time.

"Yes, it was the best fuck of my life too. I don't know if baby dreams mean that you are with child, because I once read in a dream book that it means troubles, but you are very connected to the life source, so if you think that you are pregnant then there is a good chance that you are. I obviously like that interpretation better than troubles, and that dream book has never been very accurate before. Maybe we should pass on the hanky panky and go straight for the pancakes?" Isaiah asked, getting out of bed and squeezing Phoebe in a firm hug.

"I think my turn-on has left the building for now," Phoebe responded, as the phone started ringing again.

It rang off and on for the next half hour, as Isaiah put together a delicious breakfast. The calls were from a number of different news agencies, including the *Associated Press, NBC, The New York Times, The Washington Post* and even her old friends at *ABC News*.

Phoebe did not want to answer their calls yet and didn't. She really did not know what she would say to them, and wanted to be in a less irritated state of mind when she did.

Chapter 14
Daniel's Story

New York is where Daniel was born in 1982 to Saul and Amy Granger. They lived in Scarsdale, just a little north of New York City, and were quite well off. He was the oldest of three kids, and being the first born was doted over by his parents. He excelled in school, especially in his English classes; had a knack for writing, unparalleled in someone of his age. He also had the ability to pick up a new language very quickly. He was what one would call a hyper-polyglot. His teachers swooned over him as well. He was popular with his schoolmates in spite of being at the top of his class. He was a handsome lad and had many girlfriends from 6th grade on, usually only lasting for the school year. He didn't play team sports, although he was a good athlete, and some of the guys on the football team teased Daniel about being a closet gay, mostly to recruit him to join them on their team. Daniel was confident of his sexuality, and laughed their comments off. Some of the players were also jealous of how the hot girls were more attracted to him than to them. They really knew that he was a heterosexual, and most of them actually liked Daniel.

He received a full scholarship to *Columbia University* in Manhattan in 2001, where he continued to excel, graduating in three years, then spending a year at *Oxford* on a *Rhodes* scholarship before returning to *Columbia* to get his doctorate in their *School of Journalism* in 2006, where he met Phoebe.

Even before graduating he was offered numerous job opportunities with different News agencies. He chose to work for *ABC News* and he quickly became their top foreign news reporter.

Because of his ability to speak many different languages he could interact with people in foreign countries, and was able to get great interviews with non English speaking leaders. He was sent all over the world. Phoebe went with him on occasion. Usually *ABC News* sent her to places in the United States, as she only spoke English and Spanish, and was prized for her ability to get lay people to feel comfortable and open up to her.

Daniel could speak Arabic, and he picked up Dari and Pashto when assigned to Afghanistan. He was even able to properly interview the Taliban leaders due to his speaking their language.

Some ISIS-K fighters kidnapped him when he was returning to his hotel from an interview with Mohammad Ashraf Ghani Ahmadzai, the president of Afghanistan. The kidnappers wanted to exchange him for some of their compatriots held captive at *Guantanamo Bay* prison. Unfortunately for them, the US armed forces were tracking a number of the leaders of ISIS in Afghanistan, and sent a drone to blow up one of the ISIS-K compounds in the Kunar province that is in the Northeast area of Afghanistan. It was the same compound that they had taken Daniel to, but fortunately he was outside the compound in an outhouse when the strike occurred. He was close enough to the building that he was knocked unconscious and had minor damages to his body in numerous places. ISIS-K thought that he had died in the blast along with the rest of their fighters. They reported this to the *ABC* news affiliate in Afghanistan that the U.S had murdered its own prominent citizen.

A local young woman who was also a nurse found him still alive, and got her brother to help her, and they moved him to their house nearby. Daniel lived with this family for a number of months. For over a year he didn't know who he was, and had lost almost all of his memory from the strong blast. Eventually, a few memories, like languages, came back to him. The nurse taking care of him and her family thought that he was also from the area perhaps, as he had a full beard and could speak their language as a native could. A boyfriend of this nurse became jealous of her attention on the good looking Daniel, and reported the stranger to the Taliban. They were not sure who he was, but they could tell he was not one of them, though obviously an Afghan, and took him as a recruit to the mountainous region of *Tora Bora*.

He had a form of *Stockholm* S*yndrome* and eventually was given more and more responsibilities. Daniel's memory was only returning in bits and pieces and he still was not knowledgeable of who he really was. His abilities to speak many languages were returning quickly however, and he helped the Taliban decipher messages that the U.S and NATO were putting out. There were no women at the compound except for some who were there to cook and clean. This did not stop Daniel for becoming involved with a young woman that cooked at the compound, who was turning him on despite wearing a chadaree, which is the Afghan term for a burka.

In order to have sex, and also because they liked each other, Daniel had to marry her, which he did. She was only 17, but that was quite common, and girls even much younger were being married to Taliban fighters. Her name was Aisha, which was the name of the favorite wife of Mohammad. It turns out that under the chadaree she was extremely beautiful.

Aisha could read and write in Pashtu, which is better than most Taliban women, who were denied going to school after elementary education. They were fed a lot of religious ideas and made to feel inferior to a man. Daniel taught Aisha English when they were alone, and she appreciated his kindness. She was quite intelligent, and seemed to also have a knack for picking up languages very easily.

He was already in charge of the computer network that the Taliban were using in the mountains near Pakistan. He taught Aisha to be his assistant. She seemed to pick up everything very quickly.

One time while they were making love he called her Phoebe. He did not know why at first, but then some of his memories of his past life with Phoebe started returning. Aisha became pregnant after about 6 months living with Daniel. The night that Aisha conceived was the best sex that they had until then.

Daniel had taught her some of the sensual and sexual ways that he enjoyed, and what he thought that she might like, being that she was a total virgin in all sensual respects. She was also a quick learner, and liked having sex with him. He sucked her pussy for the first time that night, and it drove Aisha wild with excitement. Her clitoris grew to an engorged size that it never had before. She was no longer a virgin by then, and had learned that Daniel liked it when she got on top of him and rode him like a wild horse. He used to like to be the one on top when having intercourse with Phoebe, but something had changed in him for some reason, whether due to the amnesia or to his maturation as a lover. Aisha wanted Daniel to have a great pleasurable experience too, one that was as good as the one she just had, and licked his penis with her tongue to get him moistened and really hard. She then pushed him down on the bed and got on top of him. Aisha was still really turned on, inserted his penis into her wet pussy. It felt wonderful to her. She was totally into the sensual feeling of pleasure that was cascading through her body, and knew how to transfer her sensations to his throbbing cock or vice versa, she wasn't quite sure which, if not both. Aisha was screaming like a banshee, as most of their neighbors had gone out that evening, and they were left alone at the compound, except for a few single men who were on the other side of the building. Daniel was groaning loudly too, and she felt as if they were one being, flying high in the sky. She would slow down and feel every millimeter of his penis for a while, and then speed up again and tantalize him with her pussy prowess. She was driving Daniel mad with lust and desire, and controlling his cock with her pussy in a way that she never had done before.

"I am going to take you up one more time Daniel, and then I am going to squeeze your penis with my pussy and squirt you into me like you never have been squirted before," Aisha loudly whispered, looking like the most beautiful sight that Daniel had ever seen.

And that is how she became pregnant with his child.

This wild sexual escapade somehow stimulated his memory some more. Daniel began to realize that he wasn't a Taliban. When he realized that he was an American, he didn't know if he should tell her, but decided that she would keep his secret.

Daniel had risen in the hierarchy of the group, and decided to take Aisha with him on a reconnaissance trip to Peshawar in Pakistan to supposedly get more guns, ammunition and money from Taliban supporters there that his comrades badly needed. He confided to her that he thought he may have already been married to a woman in America, but couldn't recall much detail, but that he loved her even more, and wanted her to come with him to America. The plan was that they would get on a bus and go from Peshawar to Islamabad, and then go directly to the American embassy when they got there. Aisha eagerly agreed, always having wanted to go to America.

Before they had left the compound, one of the Taliban soldiers in the group had overheard them talking in English. He did not understand what they were saying, but thought it was fishy, so he told the unit commander. The commander confronted Daniel. He knew that Daniel spoke multi languages, so Daniel did not deny the accusation; just told him that he was teaching Aisha how to speak English and also Arabic. The commander reminded him that it was better if women were uneducated, and to stop teaching her. Daniel apologized and agreed that he would only speak to her in Pashtu from then on.

The commander thought that he had solved the issue, but wasn't 100% sure. He arranged for a couple of his men to follow Daniel and Aisha when they went on their mission.

Daniel was given an old truck and a driver to obtain the military weapons. First however, they had to drive to southern Afghanistan to pick up the 55 gallon drums of opium from poppy farms that the Taliban controlled. This was how they were going to pay for the weapons. Aisha did not have to go on this first part of the trip. He returned a few days later with a large quantity of the poppy juice.

The Taliban had decided that they wanted Aisha to stay home and not accompany Daniel to Pakistan, but Daniel convinced them that she needed to go see a pre-natal doctor there who would advise her on her pregnancy. Daniel and Aisha were finally allowed to go. The Taliban commander still had them followed by two of his most trusted men. Daniel first met with their contacts in Pakistan, and procured the weapons for the opium exchange. The men watching them felt that everything was normal. However, when Daniel took his wife to see the doctor, they escaped, leaving their driver by himself. The driver told the other Taliban men that he was waiting for them outside the doctor's office, but they just never reappeared.

The commander was informed that they had escaped his men's surveillance and ordered his men to bring back Aisha alive, or not return home themselves. They were ordered to bring Daniel back dead or alive.

The Taliban soldiers went to the doctor's office and were told that Daniel and Aisha never showed. Somebody that they questioned in the area reported that he saw this handsome couple getting on a bus to Islamabad. At the same time that this was going on, the United States quickly decided to leave Afghanistan en masse.

The Taliban men followed the bus that Daniel and Aisha were on. They were waiting for Aisha and Daniel to get off the bus and go to the restroom. There were numerous stops along the way and for most of the journey they never left the bus. Finally about three quarters of the way to Islamabad they got lucky; they watched Aisha depart from the bus. All of the riders went to the rest room or at least got off the bus, for it was a longer rest stop than before. Everyone that is, but Daniel, who remained on the bus. On the way out of the bathroom the Afghans grabbed Aisha, quickly put her in their car and drove back west.

Daniel was angry and very heartbroken that Aisha did not get back on the bus. He was told by one of the bus riders that he saw the young woman friend of his get in a car with two fierce looking men. They took her back to Peshawar, reconnected with the truck and driver and the weapons, and went back to Afghanistan, which was being ruled already by the Taliban. When they returned to their *Tora Bora* headquarters, Aisha was locked in a room and not allowed to participate in any functions until she repented.

Daniel escaped death for the second time, and once he arrived in Islamabad, made his way to the American embassy. He still hadn't fully recovered his memory, but he did know for sure that he was an American. One of the embassy staff had related with Daniel before, and recognized who he was, in spite of his long beard, even though he was reportedly deceased more than three years before. They cleaned him up, shaved his long beard, and sent him to *Ramstein Airbase* for further debriefing.

At Ramstein they put him through numerous medical tests and questionings. They got enough information to put together what had happened since his disappearance.

The medical staff showed him a few old news videos when he was a reporter, and this enabled his memory to return in many regards. He realized that he really was married to two women. The staff at Ramstein told him that his family and wife had been contacted, and that he would be able to speak with them when they had finished all his tests.

Parasites aside, Daniel was in surprisingly good health. He was checked out by the *Ramstein Air Force Base* doctors, and was found to be in fairly good health. The only abnormality they found, which was common to soldiers returning from Afghanistan, was a type of one celled parasite that could eventually play havoc with the digestive system. However, it was not a disease that developed quickly, and could easily be removed by taking *Flagyl,* which was what he was given. His memory was not complete, but he did remember that he was born in New York City, went to school and worked in America, and yet had lived with the Taliban for close to three years.

The base had more fish to fry than just Daniel. Hundreds of evacuees at first, and then more, perhaps thousands, to a total of close to thirty-thousand Afghan citizens were being sent to Ramstein from the Kabul airport, where the Americans were making their final departures. Many of these were people who had helped, or family members of those who had helped the United States and other NATO armed forces defend the country against the Taliban, which now had claimed victory. They would be in serious trouble if they remained in Afghanistan, either killed, imprisoned, or indoctrinated by brutal reeducation techniques.

The conditions at the base had to be constantly expanded to house all the refugees. Makeshift tents were set up to accommodate the flood of refugees, plus the many port-a-potties for lavatory use. Many of the Afghans were unfamiliar with these, and there were numerous occasions at first of urinating and defecating inside the tents.

Daniel was asked by the base commander if he would help out and explain to the Afghans how to use the lavatories, and to help settle disputes between different families that were not getting along with each other. Daniel was invaluable to many of the refugees. He still did not remember fully what he did in America, or who his family was before living in Afghanistan, but *ABC* sent a slew of videos of his past interviews for him to watch, and his memory was becoming more complete each day. He finally could remember both of his parents, and his first wife Phoebe, whom he remembered meeting at *Columbia University*.

His parents were trying to get in touch with him since his reappearance had been announced, and the doctors finally agreed to let him talk with them via a video call.

His mother was all tears and bursting with happiness when she got to see her long lost son again via the videoconference. His father was more stoic, but also felt deeply emotional, as they talked about what had happened since they last were in touch. Daniel learned from all the information that he was given, plus his old memories continuously returning, once at Ramstein, that he was taken hostage by ISIS, and somehow survived a drone strike that killed many of the ISIS fighters. He also remembered being cared for by some Afghans before being recruited by the Taliban. He relayed this information to his parents who were already aware of much of it.

"I met a beautiful young Taliban girl, Aisha, after I had recuperated, and we fell in love almost instantly, and got married so that we could live together. My memory of the past was practically non-existent," Daniel said, and continued. "I finally realized that I was an American, and Aisha wanted to be with me, so we went together to Pakistan to escape the Taliban. They figured out what we were doing, and took her off the bus on the way to Islamabad. Now that the war is over, I hope to have her flown to the United States, so that we can be together."

"What are you going to do about Phoebe?" Amy Granger asked, not looking too thrilled with this bit of information.

"I just watched a video and saw us together. She is a beautiful woman. I still have limited recollection of Phoebe and our life together, but I do seem to recall that we were happily married. I guess I'm a bigamist, though inadvertently so. Aisha is also pregnant. I don't know. I really love Aisha now. I'm sure that I had loved Phoebe once, I just don't remember my time with her very well yet."

"That was all good for you when you did not know who you were, but you are a Jewish man and this Aisha I assume is a Muslim?" his mother nudged.

"Neither of us is religious. She will probably even convert, if we can somehow bring her over to America," Daniel nudged back.

"Well, you can at least call Phoebe. Maybe speaking with her will bring back your time together. Here is her number," Mrs. Granger said, as Daniel had to end the conversation, as he was needed for some squabble that two Afghan families were having about tent space.

"I will call her soon, and it's been really nice to see you both again. I love you," Daniel said, as he ended the conversation.

Chapter 15
Wolves Isaiah Phoebe

On hearing the news about Daniel, Phoebe was relieved and devastated at the same time. She had truly loved him, but over the past three years had mourned and mourned his untimely passing, and his reappearance did not fit into any of the boxes that she had crafted. She was now totally in love with Isaiah, and believed herself to be growing their child inside her. There was no proof yet of course, but she wanted to be with Isaiah now, more than she wanted to be with Daniel. She had no idea what Daniel would be like now, and she feared talking to him and finding out.

"I know it's not all about me, but right now I feel so vulnerable. I don't want to hurt Daniel, but I also want to be with you Isaiah, and not go back to my previous life," Phoebe said, after they had finished eating breakfast.

"I feel for you babe. I know that this is not an easy quandary to be in. At least the choice you have is better than your average predicament. Besides, you don't know what Daniel wants, till you speak with him. He could have moved on too, and found someone else by now as well. You at least know that I totally want you with me, and maybe we can use this as a reason to go higher and have better lives. So when he calls, I suggest that you speak with him. Be honest and mostly listen to his story, because I bet he has a doozy of one to tell," Isaiah lovingly responded.

"That makes me feel better. I am so lucky to have found you Isaiah. It's also lucky that the insurance company settled with me, because if they had given me the full amount, they could claim it back, now that he is alive. I think *ABC* will probably take him back too, but I guess I will have to wait till we hear his story," Phoebe responded.

The return of Daniel Granger was one of the top stories all over the news and Internet, along with the US withdrawal from Afghanistan. The fact that the dead journalist turned up, over three years later in Pakistan and was now recuperating in Germany, was a feel good story. It definitely helped offset some of the harsh news about the US withdrawal from Afghanistan, after over 20 years fighting ISIS and the Taliban there.

Isaiah took Phoebe on a walk through the forest to the den where the wolves were, which was about a mile away. He brought Phoebe over to introduce her to Rebecca, the pregnant alpha female. Rebecca was being very placid, very friendly, and licked Phoebe's hand, which was a thrilling first in both their lives.

"I named those three wolves over there: Hooey, Looey, and Dewey, last year when they were born. I think that it is time to give them proper adult names. Do you have any suggestions, Phoebe?"

"I don't know. I think that those names are just as good a trio of names as any other for adults or pups. Maybe just drop the ey, so Loo, Dew and Hoo. But I like the original cutesy names better myself." The three one year olds who were sort of napping, heard their names being mentioned, and came over to meet Isaiah's new friend. They also introduced themselves by licking her hand. They sniffed her as well, and by all accounts it appeared that they liked what she smelled like.

"These wolves are so nice. I can see why you have devoted yourself to their protection. I think that it is a terrible shame that their PR is so bad. I think I will see what I can do to help out with that," Phoebe added.

"They are more afraid of humans than anything else, and rightfully so. If you weren't with me they would not let you approach like this, and would probably have remained hidden, and ran away. Now that they know you to be a friend, they will be loyal, and treat you accordingly," Isaiah said, as he came up to Phoebe and held her in a gentle embrace, and kissed her cheeks in a loving manner.

He could feel that sensation starting up again in his loins, and at the same time the three one year olds howled in harmony. This woke up the alpha male Barack, and also his brother and sister, Antonio, and Pippa, who were sleeping a good distance away on top of a ridge. They also came over to introduce themselves to Phoebe. Phoebe felt welcomed now by the entire pack.

It was a lovely moment out in the wilderness. Phoebe momentarily forgot about the earlier events, and felt that blissful space of feeling the pleasure of being alive, being present in the moment, and not the suffering from over thinking, especially about what to do and what to say to Daniel.

Phoebe and Isaiah stayed together for the rest of the week, and for the beginning of the following week. She loved the way he respected and treated her, and gave her space when she needed it. They had frequent extremely fun sensual experiences together, interspersed with some soul searching that Phoebe had to process.

Daniel had been charming and generous when they had been together, but was a bit full of himself, though he did have good reasons to be so, being so intelligent, but not really wise, Phoebe thought. He was more than a bit of a womanizer, and had partaken in a number of affairs, mostly hookers or sex workers as they are called now, when he was abroad only. She had forgiven him those indiscretions, as he told her about them right after they happened, and they did have a somewhat open marriage, even though Phoebe was faithful on her end, until she thought he had died. Sometimes, some of the new kinky stuff he learned he would bring back to their marriage to share. He explained that his affairs were only to relieve his sexual energies when he was away from her. When they were together he was totally faithful, and kept his full attention on her.

She expected that Daniel would be calling her at any time, but the call had not materialized. On the following Wednesday she finally heard from Daniel's mother Amy. Amy told her that she had just spoken to Daniel and informed her of the mental state of her son. He had amnesia when he was injured from the bomb blast, and only now was putting together his memories. She didn't tell Phoebe that he still couldn't recall much of his time with her, but she did mention about his Muslim wife being pregnant with his child. She also told Phoebe that she had given Daniel her number, and that he promised to call her.

Amy was surprised that Phoebe received that bit of information without becoming angry, but figured that Phoebe was probably just happy that Daniel was still alive.

Phoebe thought that this new bit of information just made her decision to be with Isaiah easier, and was really relieved to hear that Daniel had found someone else.

"Guess what Isaiah?" Phoebe said, being in a noticeably better mood than when she had first realized who was calling her.

"You won the lottery?" Isaiah mused.

"Better than that. You were right. Daniel got married in Afghanistan and he wants to bring his pregnant bride over to the United States, and take care of her and his child. This changes everything, I think. I won't have to reject him now, he can reject me, and I can play the victim. Amy Granger, his mother, just gave him my number; said that he will call me soon."

"Well, aren't you the lucky one now, getting me as your first choice," Isaiah joked. "I hope he doesn't want to start a harem with her and you," Isaiah continued with the levity.

"That is possible, not such a joke. He did take a number of different women to bed when we were married, but those

Jezebels were all overseas, he assured me. Anyhow, that is an easy one to decline, even though I know you meant it as a joke. It really isn't that far fetched, knowing Daniel, or at least the Daniel that I knew," Phoebe responded.

"Hmm, that I didn't know. Wolves don't have harems, and I am in agreement with them. It's one alpha male and one alpha female and the others do not usually breed. Speaking of which, I have a gut feeling that today is the day Rebecca is going to give birth. I checked on her early this morning and she looked ready, and was heading into the den," Isaiah said.

"This is truly a good omen day. Maybe we can name the pups, Nell Gwynn, Cora Pearl and Lulu White, 3 famous prostitutes if they are female; and King Henry, King Louis and King Charles for men, who were connoisseurs of sex workers," Phoebe quipped.

"That's funny, if one of the pups is a white wolf, we can name it Whitey. King is a good wolf name and I like both Lulu and Nelly too," Isaiah answered.

Just then Phoebe's phone rang. It was Daniel.

"Wow, it is you. Your voice sounds the same, Daniel. I was so happy to hear that you are alive. It is such a miracle, believing that you were dead for almost 4 years," Phoebe greeted him with some genuine fond emotion, but not tipping her hand.

"Yes, I am alive. I never thought that I was dead, but I have been finding so many old memories that had once been me, which felt like they had died and have now been resurrected. Even speaking with you now brings me closer to who I was. Your voice reminds me of who you are or were. Honestly, I hadn't remembered much about our life together, until the doctors showed me some old videos of us, and after just speaking with my mom and dad. I'm putting together, or somehow regaining what I used to be. They say that eventually I will be able to remember almost everything. I know now that we were once in love, and married," Daniel said, and continued.

"You may have heard that I got married again to a Taliban girl. She was there for me when I was recovering and after. Since I did not know who I was, I was recruited and willingly helped the Taliban, till I recently realized that I was an American, and was duped into helping them. They treated me justly, as they didn't know who I was either, and I should probably call it something else besides duped. Anyhow I am now a bigamist. I love Aisha, but she is still over in Afghanistan. I want to try and bring her over here. She is pregnant, and I want to do the honorable thing by her. I also want to do the honorable thing by you. It is quite the dilemma. Anyhow, I am currently helping the soldiers here in Ramstein get this evacuee problem handled, and I should be returning to the United States before too long, and hope to meet with you when I do. I will probably first stay with my parents in Scarsdale when I get back. Where are you now living Phoebe?"

"I was mourning you for over three years. I moved out to California as soon as I heard you had died, to be with my family here. I recently bought a house of my own, not too far from where they live," Phoebe answered.

"Maybe you can come out to Scarsdale, or I could visit you in California. We could possibly rekindle our relationship. We are probably still married under the law, as we never got divorced, right?" Daniel asked.

Phoebe's heart sank and then resurfaced. It is nice to be wanted, but her heart now belonged to Isaiah. I've changed, she thought. It seems Daniel may have forgotten his life, but still is the same person inside.

"I am actually in love again for the first time since you've been gone. I have feelings for you of course, but I am happy now with my new partner Isaiah. You and I are no longer legally married any more. Once a spouse is presumed deceased, the marriage is over. I am sure that I will want to see you eventually, but I think it is best for me and for you to act like we are split up. I hope you don't mind my being so blunt, but this way you can put your attention on bringing your wife and baby to be with you. Are you going to work for *ABC* again?" Phoebe then asked, after deciding not to pull her punches, and to then change the topic of conversation.

"I am already doing a special for *ABC* here in Germany about the Afghan evacuees. They've sent out a camera crew and it is going to play on *20/20* next week. They are also doing a special on me that will be part of the show. A heads up, someone from *20/20* may be calling you for an interview for that. I am actually glad for you that you found someone. I think true love is wanting those you love to be happy and to fulfill their life purpose," Daniel answered proudly and surprisingly magnanimously.

"I am so glad that you feel that way. I want the best for you as well. I don't know if I want to be on TV again though. I do look forward to seeing you on the small screen, even though they are not so small any more. Maybe next time we can actually do a video call on the real small phone screen," Phoebe responded, ending the conversation a bit lightheartedly.

"Well, that didn't go as well as I had hoped, but better than it could have gone. I guess you heard what Daniel said. I kept it on speaker phone so you wouldn't feel left out," Phoebe related to Isaiah.

"Thank you for including me. That was a good and honest response you gave him about the marriage being over for you. He seems like a nice enough person, though as you say, a bit full of himself, even though he doesn't even know all of himself yet," Isaiah responded.

"You are welcome, and the thanks really is from me to you. Do you think that I should do the interview that he mentioned?" Phoebe asked.

"That is up to you. I really don't care one way or the other. You did seem very comfortable in front of the camera when I used to watch your reports," Isaiah answered.

"Thanks for the input, even though I think I would have liked you to say a definite yes or a definite no, instead of not caring one way or the other. I still would make the final decision, but your viewpoint would be helpful," Phoebe said.

"Let's go see how Rebecca is doing," Isaiah said, changing the subject, not particularly liking where their conversation was headed.

"That I definitely would like. Let me put my shoes and jacket on and we can go," Phoebe declared.

"I like your definite yes on that," Isaiah joked, as they headed out the door.

Rebecca was inside the den when they got to the wolves' turf. The other wolves were milling about. Barack was parading in front of the den with his chest expanded, as a sure sign of a proud dad. They could hear the sounds of the newborn pups whimpering and hiccuping from inside the den.

"I wish we could see them," Phoebe stated.

"Actually we can. I have a secret video camera inside the den. I can turn the feed on, and we can check them out on my phone," Isaiah stated, as he did some clicking actions on his *IPhone*. He then held it up so they both could see inside the den.

"Wow, they are so tiny and so cute. It is quite dark in there, and their fur seems dark too. No whiteys, I thought they would be bigger. I think I see three of them. It looks like two of them are already sucking on Rebecca, and she is licking the third one. It looks like his eyes are closed," Phoebe remarked.

"Yes, they are only one pound or so at birth, but they grow rapidly. Pups are deaf and blind with closed eyes for about a week after being born. Then when they open them, their eyes are a deep blue. Their eyes don't remain blue for long, and between 6-8 weeks they develop into their permanent colors that can be anywhere from golden yellow, amber, orange, or even a green color. Some wolf pups may even grow to have light gray eyes, which can be mistaken for blue eyes from a distance. Most pups have dark fur when they are born, just like these. Many times the fur will lighten as they grow older," Isaiah stated in a short tutorial.

"They are adorable. As you know I have to go back south today. I want to see a realtor about renting out my home, so I can come back here and be with you. Maybe before I leave, you could possibly give me an orgasm, hint hint. It will make the drive much more pleasurable," Phoebe said, as Isaiah could feel that stirring in his loins.

Phoebe looked at Isaiah with her full intention and attention. They were back in his cabin that he had started to warm up with another log on the fire. He looked back at her eyes with an equal amount of purpose and desire. He slowly approached Phoebe and put his hands behind her back and pulled her up against his body. She felt delicious in his arms. He stroked her long dark hair behind her head, at times touching lightly the soft hairs, and then switching to more pressure upon her scalp where the roots of her hair lay. Her mouth was partly parted, and he gazed at her beautiful face from close-up.

"You get more beautiful every time I look at you Phoebe. You have put some love spell on me that creates so much beauty in my vision," Isaiah said, as he put his own slightly parted lips against hers. He kissed her gently at first, hardly moving his mouth, and just feeling his own lips tingling from their connection, which were sending electric jolts continuously into his body.

Phoebe was feeling a similar response in her body, and they held this embrace for some time. Then Isaiah started probing her lips with the tip of his tongue. Phoebe was feeling every iota of sensation that Isaiah was initiating. He could feel her lips becoming engorged and he pressed against them with incremental increases in pressure and movement. It felt like she sucked his tongue inside her mouth and engaged it with her own tongue in a glorious sensual dance. The kiss, magnificent from the start, became even more and more passionate as it continued for several minutes. Isaiah could feel his penis against Phoebe's body becoming fully erect. He had the thought that it was time to take her to bed and stroke her naked skin, and give her that orgasmic send-off that she asked for.

He kept kissing her and moved their engaged bodies to the side of the bed; pushing her back onto the mattress with her legs bent, and her feet still touching the floor. He lay sort of on top of her with his legs between hers, and continued devouring her mouth with his. She was giving as well as she was getting, and they both were in absolute physical bliss.

Isaiah finally separated himself from lying on top of Phoebe, including retrieving his tongue, which he reluctantly did, and he used it to talk, and said, "That was an amazing kiss Phoebe. Your mouth is such a soft, luscious, and sensational place to be. That was the best kiss of my life once again. Now for your reward, I'm going to remove your pants and have my way with your pussy."

"That was the best kiss I ever had as well. The jolts of sensation that emanated from the touching of our lips was more than superb," Phoebe exclaimed, and letting Isaiah remove her pants and panties, tingling with pleasure all over her body.

Isaiah placed a pillow on the floor between her naked legs, and kneeled down stretching his arms to fondle and stimulate her breasts and nipples. He put his head between her thighs and inhaled deeply. "I love the way your pussy smells. Your fragrance is as perfect as you are beautiful. I am now going to taste your upper thighs and work my way to your pussy," he exclaimed.

Then he put his head back between her naked legs and started kissing her inner thighs and tasting them with his tongue. He approached her pussy, pressed and pulled up on her lower abdomen, while pulling apart her labia with both hands, to expose her vulva. He moved her pubic hair out of the way and licked her wet introitus from bottom to top, stopping just short of her clitoris. Phoebe was gasping with pleasure. He continued licking her labia, her introitus, and perineum, when she asked him to lick her clitoris too. Isaiah stopped for a second. He told her that he would get there in good time, which was a few strokes later, after he started again. Isaiah then began to gently lick Phoebe's clitoris with the tip of his tongue, up and down, and then back down to her labia, and then swirling his tongue to her exposed clitoris for a few intense licks.

"That is so intense and wonderful," Phoebe remarked, throbbing with pleasure.

"That was really fun. You are so wet, and your contractions were stupendous. I could feel your contractions vibrating in my own body. You are my prisoner now, and I am going to pull you all the way onto the bed, and use my hands to continue pleasuring you," Isaiah said, as he got up and pulled Phoebe by her shoulders all the way onto the bed, so that she lay perpendicularly on it.

"Please take off your pants too. I want to see your cock while you are touching my pussy," Phoebe politely requested.

Isaiah agreed to her request. He sat on her left side with her pussy easily available to his hands, so that he could also see what he was doing, as he sat crosswise to her supine body. His right leg was over her belly and his left leg was under her legs, which were spread apart for easy access. Because she was already in orgasm, he did not have to tease her to get her full attention. He placed his left hand, with fingers spread evenly, under her buttocks, with his thumb resting gently but assuredly at the base of her vaginal opening. He put a bit of lubricant on his right index finger tip. Her clitoris was already engorged from his mouth, and he put his lubricated finger right on her spot on the upper left side of her clitoris.

The contractions began immediately again. "Ah, that feels so good," Phoebe kept saying over and over, while Isaiah gave her a steady diet of short light strokes.

She turned her head to take a look at his crotch, and could see that he was engorged as well, his penis actually rubbing up against her thigh and buttock area. "Can I put my hand on your cock," Phoebe asked in a moaning voice?

"Not yet, I will let you know. I am in charge here," Isaiah responded, giving her some longer strokes, and then getting back on her spot.

"Okay, just tell me when. You've got really great hands. Ah, ah, you got me so. I am yours and only yours," Phoebe exclaimed, as she kept on contracting with her extended, and quite massive orgasm.

Isaiah kept taking her higher and higher. There was one point where she let out a loud moan. "Your finger right there on my spot is the best ever. Oh God, it keeps going up. Right there, that is the best. I am so high," Phoebe proclaimed, as if she was seeing God for the first time.

Continuing to peak Phoebe, and then take her to the next level, Isaiah was having the time of his life. He was probably doing this for over half an hour, and he finally said, "Okay Phoebe, you can touch my penis now, but don't forget you are still my prisoner."

Phoebe had been watching his erect penis while he stroked her pussy, and noticed that it too was oozing small amounts of semen for the past several minutes, even getting her thigh coated with some. She gently put her left hand on it, and it felt so good in her hand that her pussy exploded to the next level. She had been giving up control to Isaiah, but after that last burst in her pussy, she had felt filled up with all the pleasure that she could consume at that moment, and wanted to play with his magnificent toy.

"I am taking over now," Phoebe declared, as she maneuvered his body into a prone position with his head lifted on a pillow so he could watch her sexy body, as she began to take over the controls.

"No, you can't do this to me. You are my prisoner," Isaiah repeated, but with less fortitude.

She sat between his legs and put her legs over his. He could see her face and her pussy staring directly at him. She put some lubricant on his penis and coated it all around his throbbing member, and started stroking his penis with two hands, one following the other. She lightened up toward his corona on the way up his penis. Phoebe then used increasingly more pressure on the way down, pressing firmly against his pubic area. She then ascended his very long shaft again, using lighter pressure the further up his penis she stroked, and down again in a steady rhythm. Phoebe was taking Isaiah for a personal sensual party, one hand and then the other, up and down his long shaft.

"Your cock feels so magnificent in my hand. You are my prisoner now. So surrender my dear," Phoebe stated, although in reality, Isaiah had already surrendered. "It is so big, and seems to continue to grow larger with lots of throbbing and oozing," Phoebe shared. She changed the stroke to a more spiral twisting motion that had Isaiah gasping for air.

"Oh Phoebe, that feels so tremendous. You sure have shown me some of your tricks, as you promised. Your pussy watching over me, and your sexual onslaught is so enticing," Isaiah was able to blurt out between gasps of pleasure.

"Who is the prisoner now Mr.? You are mine," Phoebe teased, as she continued her assault. "I got you right there," as she pulled his testicles towards her and up away from his body, and stroked his shaft and the part of his shaft that was inside his body under his testicles. "There is no escape. I will do what I please to you," as she pulled on his penis with authority and love.

This was more than Isaiah had ever felt before. His moans were becoming louder and louder, and his cock was still getting longer. Phoebe was working his genitals like an expert who has trained for years harvesting her skills. She had him at the edge and seemed to know exactly when to back off, and when to start again, to keep him at the edge. She lingered over the head of his penis, and slowly twisted her fingers around it to bring him even higher to the next level that had him squealing with delight. She was dominating his cock, as Hillary and Tensing Norgay had conquered Everest.

Still stroking him, Phoebe got closer and closer with her pussy to his giant penis, and finally inserted it into her still very wet vagina to finish him off. She gymnastically got on top of him and rode him up and down until he could not take it any longer, and he exploded into her pussy with all the force of a violent volcano erupting in a series of strong powerful heaves, with earth shattering energies that she felt throughout every cell of her body. All their energies were converted into a plethora of pleasures.

After a couple of minutes of total silence following the eruption, Isaiah finally said, "That was amazing. No, it was better than amazing. I don't know the words. Super amazing maybe, even that falls short. I think that may fill you up for your trip home Phoebe, don't you think?" Isaiah exclaimed, with a giant grin beaming from one side of his face to the other side.

Phoebe slid off her stallion. "I think I must be two pounds heavier after that. If I wasn't pregnant before, I sure will be now. That was the best for me too. By far the best fuck. Your cock filled me up so that it felt as if it was inside every inch and cell of my body. It felt like we were one giant united body. I never had so much fun with a penis before, and as you know, I am no virgin," Phoebe bellowed, as she went into the bathroom to clean up, and freshen up for her ride back south. Isaiah slowly went into the kitchen to make her a portobello mushroom sandwich for her drive back to the Bay area.

Phoebe felt that she was floating back home instead of driving. It all felt effortless, and she was driving in that special zone where all was perfect, until her phone rang, and brought her back to reality. It was Rachel of course.

"You said that you would get back to me, and it's been almost two weeks since we talked, so I decided to call you anyway," Rachel stated.

"I know. A lot has been going on. I have spoken with Daniel, and he is coming back to the States this week or next from Germany. He has a new Taliban wife, as you probably heard, but she is still in Afghanistan. He says he is okay with us being divorced, but then he also wants to get together. Daniel said that he is coming out to California to see his sister, and to see me soon. I also know that I am pregnant by Isaiah, even though it has only been a couple weeks since we first had sex. It was so good. I want to have his baby, and I want to be with him. I feel so happy around him. He is so loving and nurturing, and wild at the same time. I am on my way back to the Bay area now. I just had the best fuck of my life, even better than that earlier great one. You won't believe what a great lover he is, and he brings out the wild animal in me. He sucked and licked and rubbed on my pussy for quite some time. I was coming like a banshee. He really knows his way around my clitoris. He knows exactly what spot feels the best and when to stroke it. He stops right before I have had enough, and then starts again, taking me even higher."

"Wow, slow down. That is a mouthful," Rachel interrupted.

"Okay, I'll try. Isaiah would not allow me to touch him until I was totally ravished. I then took over and became the aggressor. I had him real good too. Once I twirled my hand around his corona he was screaming for sexual mercy. His penis feels so exquisite, I can still feel it now. Then I got on top of him and rode him like a wild stallion. It was insane. I had so much control over him. We were both moaning like there was no tomorrow. Daniel usually wanted to be the one on top, and I often let him. This was so much more fun for me, and I think for Isaiah as well. I could feel his big cock filling up every space in my body, and when I exploded his juices into my pussy, it felt like the *Hoover Dam* had burst, sending tons of liquids into me."

"You are one lucky girl, *Hoover Fucking Dam*! I am happy for you. Does Isaiah have any brothers? I had my date with the online guy. He was okay, but he definitely is not the one. I am so jealous that you have two great guys wanting you. I don't think I will see this guy again, but there is another guy on the dating app who I will be checking out tonight. We had a *FaceTime* chat and he is handsome and clever, hopefully not too clever. What are you going to do with Daniel when he visits?"

"Isaiah does not have any brothers. I don't know what I will do with Daniel. I'm hoping that he stays in New York. But knowing him, he will want what he has been told that he cannot have. The past two weeks have been a whir. I am going to rent my home, and move into Isaiah's rustic cabin. I will feminize and gentrify it some, but it is basically quite comfortable, and the surroundings could hardly be more beautiful. He said that he will build a room for the baby, and even a guest room, though he is not as sure as I am that one is on the way," Phoebe said, before Rachel could get another word in edgewise.

"I am really so happy for you. Maybe some of your lucky pussy juice will spill over to me. Drive safely, and I will speak to you soon," Rachel said, ending the conversation.

For most of the ride home, Phoebe remained in that blissful zone. The ride went quickly. Phoebe felt fully connected with Isaiah.

Phoebe's mother texted her as she was approaching the Bay area, to let her know that she and her husband wanted to take her out for dinner whenever she got back to Marin. Phoebe knew that her mother would be taking the opposite side on the Daniel/Isaiah matter, but Phoebe also knew where she firmly stood, and felt she had to communicate her desires to her mother sooner or later. Besides, she was hungry, and they ate at good restaurants. Phoebe also knew that she would not remain in that cloud nine zone forever, so she could intentionally release it, knowing that she could get back there again that much sooner, if she acted deliberately.

Chapter 16
Daniel

Powerfully, Daniel's memories stopped coming back one at a time. They were now flooding into and out of his brain all at once. It was both invigorating and kind of scary. He now fully remembered the life he had before he went to and was almost killed in Afghanistan. He used to host a nighttime report called *Granger in Danger*, the last one right before he was kidnapped. He had originally thought that it was a cute title, but it turned out to be a bit too accurate, if not ominous.

He remembered being kidnapped and going to the so called unsafe safe-house with the ISIS commandoes, and watching the compound explode from a missile that was fired from a drone. He even remembered the whistling sound it made. He remembered being nursed back to health by a compassionate young woman and her kind family, and then being taken to *Tora Bora* by the Taliban, who no longer knew who he was. Most of all, he now remembered Phoebe, and the wonderful life they had built together. He wanted her back.

He did a magnificent interview at Ramstein for *20/20*, being portrayed as an American hero. They showed clips from his earlier TV shows, plus recent video footage from his helping out at the air base facilitating so many Afghan families. He confided to the interviewer that he loved both his wives, and his biggest upcoming decisions after retuning back home involved straightening out his connubial conundrum. Phoebe had decided not to take part in the show.

His interview was watched almost all over the world on *ABC,* and then it was replayed on *U-Tube* and went mega-viral. Aisha was able to watch the show on the Internet, which instigated a powerful feeling of bravado that had her try to rejoin him as soon as she could in any way possible.

Since the Taliban had taken over and now ruled the country, her services as a computer software operative and language translator for the fighters was no longer crucial, and a very pregnant woman was not a top priority to them. She had recently been moved to a Kabul address, and was allowed more freedom than before, though they still kept tabs on her. She was finally able to reach Daniel in Germany from her friend's phone, after numerous failed attempts. This was what Daniel was waiting for. He told her to go to the Qatar embassy, as they were representing American interests in Afghanistan. Daniel knew many important politicians and diplomats, and it was not difficult to get Aisha out of Afghanistan. He would arrange for her to get a special flight out of the country through his contacts at the State Department. He told her to wait a couple of weeks in Qatar, so that he could meet her in New York, since he had not made it all the way home yet himself, and there was no need for her to go to Germany first.

After the arrangements were made, it took about a week for Aisha to get out of Afghanistan. She first took refuge at the embassy of the Gulf nation of Qatar, who had already been informed by the American State Department to expedite her removal. She was flown to *Al Udeid Air Force Base,* southwest of Doha, Qatar, almost immediately. The base was home to a number of coalition forces, plus the Qatar Air Force. Once there, she was given a room on the base. There were hundreds of other Afghans staying on the base, in makeshift barracks and tents, waiting to move on. Aisha was able to help translate for some of the non English speaking refugees, just as Daniel had been doing in Germany. After medically checking her out for over a week, she was approved to fly to the United States. Aisha was in good health, in spite of being pregnant.

Aisha was flown to *Dulles International Airport* in Virginia and then transported with some other refugees to *McGuire-Dix-Lakehurst Air Force Base* in New Jersey.

A few days before she arrived, Daniel was also allowed to go home. He was picked up by his parents and was staying with them in Scarsdale. The reunion was rather emotional, especially for his mother. His folks understandably had also watched his interview before he arrived, and already had known about his two wives. They did not know that his Muslim wife was going to arrive shortly. They had adored Phoebe, and thought that she was the perfect trophy wife, plus she also happened to be extremely capable in her own right.

When Daniel related that he was going to go to New Jersey to pick up Aisha, they did not say anything out loud, but one could feel their spirits becoming deflated all the same.

Daniel got a driver from *ABC News* to chauffeur him to the base, where he was received by a Lieutenant Jennings, as a celebrity, which he was, and even more so after his interview. Aisha was delivered to him almost immediately. They hugged one another and they got in the back of the *Mercedes* Limousine. He noticed how huge her belly had become, despite her wearing a burqa.

"It's so great to be with you again Daniel," Aisha said in perfect English, once they were on their way, holding his hand on her lap.

"Yes, I have missed you tremendously too. You look a lot more pregnant than I remember, even with your burqa on. It's not a bad maternity outfit, but I think it would be best if you dressed like everyone else does in America. How soon are we expecting?" Daniel asked.

"It's still about two and a half months away, but the doctor at the base did an exam and told me that I was carrying twins, a boy and a girl."

"That's wonderful," Daniel gulped, as his own belly did a bit of a flop.

"I don't really have any western outfits, but I think it would be way easier to blend in, then to stand out in your country as a Muslim. You will have to take me shopping then," Aisha spoke calmly.

"Good, though I am no expert on clothing, but I can have one of the wardrobe girls, or even my mother take you out to some stores like *Saks Fifth Avenue, Bloomingdales*, or even *Bergdorf Goodman*. You can get some stuff for expectant mothers, plus some outfits for later, after the delivery. It will be fun to get to see your face more often." Daniel laughed.

The Grangers came out to greet their new daughter in law, as the limousine pulled up to their horseshoe driveway. They thought she probably could not speak English very well, and were much surprised when Aisha spoke in a perfect American, or even New York accent, to tell them how happy she was to meet them. She even asked them about the baseball *Yankees*, football *Giants* and *Jets,* and even the *Knicks* and *Rangers*, which were the New York teams that they rooted for. Daniel had coached her on the way there. They could not help but like her, and they were really impressed as to how beautiful she was, despite being pregnant. Daniel asked his mother if she had any clothes that Aisha could wear, so that she could get out of her Burqa. Amy gave her a couple outfits that Bella left at the house. Daniel took Aisha to his room upstairs while his parents waited downstairs.

Bella was actually flying in from California. She wanted to see her reborn brother again, and also wanted to meet his new bride. She showed up shortly after Daniel and Aisha had come, and was there to see them come down the stairs. She was so happy to see her brother again that she did not even mind when she noticed this beautiful dark haired and olive skinned young woman wearing her old loose fitting clothes, though they were quite tight on this present physique. She gave her big brother a huge hug, and also hugged Aisha. Daniel asked Bella if she would take Aisha shopping, or if he should get one of the wardrobe girls to do it, as she had brought hardly anything with her. After asking Bella, Daniel realized that his sister may not be the best person in the world for Aisha to hang out with, as she was so self centered, but it was too late, as Bella eagerly agreed to take her into the city the next day.

The three of them took the train into New York City the following day. Daniel was to go meet some of the executives at *ABC* to discuss how they were going to use him next, while the two young ladies went shopping.

Chapter 17
Phoebe Isaiah Daniel

Quandaries aside, Phoebe was in a great mood. She had gotten everything in order. She found a nice young couple to rent her home. She had contacted the *National Geographic TV* network, specifically one of the producers for the *National Geographic Wild* or *NGW,* that she had been friends with at *ABC,* who now worked for *NGW*. She pitched them her idea about doing an episode on the return of the *California Gray Wolf*. They eagerly agreed. She had gotten the okay from Isaiah and asked him to set up cameras, especially around the den, so that they could video the first appearance of the cubs. She would reimburse him for his expenses, as she was allowed a good sum of money to do the hour long show.

Phoebe also missed her period. She took a pregnancy test shortly thereafter. She did not really have to look at the results. It was firmly positive as she knew it would be. Phoebe immediately called Isaiah.

"Guess what daddy?" she began the conversation.

"Wow, really? That is so cool. You knew it right away too. I'm impressed. I thought you were maybe putting your hopes before your reality, but no, you were living your hopes and reality at the same time," Isaiah responded enthusiastically.

"And if it's triplets, we know what to call them," Phoebe joshed.

"You don't know that yet, do you? I'd believe anything you tell me now. By the way, I bought and set up three motion responding video cameras that integrate with my computer. I put them at different angles to get a number of distinct views you can choose from. The pups have not appeared yet, but they will soon. Meanwhile the rest of the pack had been tripping the motion responders, and we have a bunch of footage already," Isaiah bragged.

"That's wonderful news; I also rented my place for the first of the month, which is next week already, so I will be able to join you soon, once I tie up all my loose ends. I heard that Daniel's wife Aisha has joined him at his parent's mansion in Scarsdale. She is expecting twins. I think Daniel's sister Bella flew out to be with him too," Phoebe said, filling Isaiah in on the latest events.

"Great, I'm glad that he is busy and not pestering you. I heard from Hootman, and he is retiring at the end of the year. He has offered me his job, plus his recommendation to teach at the University, and a share of his business. It would mean moving to Montana though, so it is something we have to discuss," Isaiah offered.

"Hmm, Montana, I don't know. Maybe it would be good. We will have to think about that. Do you have a time frame that you have to respond by? It's further away from our family, but the University is there in Missoula. We would be in or closer to a civilized city in Missoula, so maybe it would be a good idea. Perhaps it would be a better place to bring up our triplets," Phoebe responded laughingly.

"Hootman said that I can have 3 months to make up my mind. I also told him about you. He had only nice things to say about you Phoebe, and would love for you to come too of course." Isaiah added.

"Well, you can tell him that if you do come there, you are only going to come with me, and also that I fondly remember him," Phoebe emphasized.

"Also, I got a call from Dannie, the blond girl at Bolinas Beach, the one with the malamute. She asked if she could visit us and have a threesome," Phoebe added.

"What? Are you kidding me? Do you think I had to be reminded of which blond girl from Bolinas? What did you tell her?" Isaiah asked, sounding perhaps more interested than Phoebe expected, but pleasantly so to her.

"I told her that you probably wouldn't be interested, but that I'd ask you anyhow. I'm kidding. I just told her I would let her know after we spoke," Phoebe teased.

"Whatever you think is right. But just talking to you about it, I can feel sensual sensations cascading through my body, as if my blood was carbonated," Isaiah said, which to Phoebe sounded like an endorsement.

"I'll tell Dannie that her idea was effervescent to you, and to think of some fun ménage a trois scenarios we could do. Maybe we two girls can do some kissing while you play with the doggy ha ha. Dannie can join us on the first weekend of next month, after I get up there. I wouldn't want the three of you up there without me," Phoebe laughingly said.

"You are funny, I think. I'll do whatever the two of you want. I have never been with two women at once before, so I'll leave it up to you," Isaiah remarked.

"Do you think I have? This is all new to me too. I'm just ready to have as much fun with what comes along as I can, and I've chosen you Isaiah to be my partner in crime, so let's open some new vistas on the pleasure circuit when they present themselves. Okay?" Phoebe said with genuine love for Isaiah enveloping him, even from long distance.

"I so look forward to having you up here full time. I am game to whatever you desire, and a threesome with Dannie seems not a difficult choice for me to say yes to," Isaiah responded, returning the envelope of love to its sender.

Phoebe's mother Karen, of course wanted her to go back with Daniel, rather than a wild man in the woods, as she called him. When Phoebe told her mother that she was pregnant with the wild man's baby, her mother became a lot more agreeable and nicer towards Isaiah, even though she still had not met him, and started calling him by his given name.

Daniel called her up too. Phoebe also confided to him that she was pregnant. That did not deter him from wanting her back, nor the fact that Aisha was with him now in the United States.

"Wouldn't it be nice if we all lived together in a large house somewhere. You and Aisha could become friends. When I went off to do a story somewhere, you would have each other to keep company. She is going to have twins a few months before you are due. We could bring up all the kids together. Think about it. I don't want you to answer me right now. I haven't told her about this idea yet either, but she will do whatever I want. She was brought up to obey men, plus having a harem is not new to her religion. Islamic law allows men to take up to four wives. Muhammad had 13 wives. He was monogamous with his first wife Kadija. They were married for 25 years, and only after she died at age 50 did he start building a harem. Think about it," Daniel said again.

"I don't really have to think about it, but I will bring it up to Isaiah anyhow. I love Isaiah now, the father of my baby. He is a good man. I will tell him about your ideas, Mr. Prophet. He is into wolves and tending to the wilderness. I don't think that he would want to live communally, especially in a suburban neighborhood, but there are some benefits to living with other folks, so I will let you know," Phoebe said, in too good a mood to let Daniel bring her down.

Daniel did a little detective work and found out some information about Isaiah. He saw some photos of him on Facebook and noticed that he was black. He was quite light for a black man, but enough black that he knew that Phoebe's mother would not want an interracial marriage for her daughter. Daniel himself did not think of himself as a racist, but he was willing to pull out the race card when it came to getting Phoebe back. He decided to call up Phoebe's mother Karen. He knew that she was a bit of a racist, if one could be a bit of that.

"Hi Karen, this is Daniel, back from the dead. How are you doing?"

"Fine, I was so glad to hear that you survived and are back in the United States. I saw your interview and you still look great, and have that same small screen magnetism that you always had. How are you? I was disappointed that you got remarried. I was hoping that you and Phoebe could resume your marriage again," Karen responded.

"I am okay. All my old memories came back, first slowly, then recently, sort of all at once. Have you met Phoebe's new boyfriend? I heard that he grew up in Marin, and played football under his grandfather Ben Williams, who was one of the first black coaches in the Bay area."

"No, I have not met her new boyfriend yet. She seems to be head over heels about him. I don't quite understand it. She is such a special and talented person and here she is falling in love with a guy who lives in the woods," Karen responded.

"It is hard to understand, but she was probably lonely. I saw his profile on *Facebook*. He is quite handsome, a bit younger than she is. I have offered her to resume our marriage, or at least to live together. My new wife would love to meet her, and even live together. I'll keep asking Phoebe. Sooner or later she will probably tire of being out in some cabin in the woods without any civilization around," Daniel stated.

"Thanks for remembering me. I will do what I can to have Phoebe see what would be in her best interest. I don't think this guy is right for her, if you know what I mean," Karen said.

"It was good to hear your voice again. Give my best regards to your husband Frank. You can call me any time. Bye," Daniel smiled, as he turned off his phone.

Daniel felt guilty right after making that call. It's true he wanted Phoebe back, but he didn't want to cause her any suffering either. He did not have anything against this Isaiah fellow, besides the fact that Phoebe had fallen in love with him. He actually believed that black Americans had received more than their fair share of suffering over the past 400 years in America, and did not want this negative karma freebasing on his conscious.

He decided to call Phoebe and explain what he had done, to ease his guilt. "Hi Phoebe, it's me again. I wanted to confess a bitchy thing that I just did. I called your mother and snuck in the fact that Isaiah was a black American. I felt awful after doing so, and wanted to warn you that she might try to dissuade you from moving in with him. Please forgive me Phoebes," Daniel declared, with honest remorse emanating over the electronic connection.

"Oh, thanks Daniel for letting me know. I really do not put much stock in what my mother wants me to do. She was going to find out about Isaiah sooner or later anyhow. I've grown up some since you and I have parted, and I am more of an independent thinker now. I only do what I want to do, and feel is best for me, as long as it doesn't hurt anyone's spiritual awareness. If it hurts their ego, then maybe they will either grow from it or not, but I am not going to change my behavior to console their egos. I can easily forgive you your faux pas, if that is what it was. We all do foolish things in the name of love. It just means that you are willing to be an arse to try and get me back, so it is kind of flattering in an unseemly way. I am soon on my way to move in with Isaiah, and I truly hope that you and he can behave like gentlemen, and perhaps even become friends, for my sake. You are a good person Daniel, and don't worry about my mother. I can handle her bullshit," Phoebe responded piquantly.

"I am glad that you are so forgiving, and I really want you to be happy. I appreciate your honesty, and your forthrightness. My disappearance must have been really hard on you, probably harder than what I went through, because my memories were not available to cause me suffering. Please stay in touch. Just hearing your voice has me feel better. Thanks again for your understanding. I love you dearly," Daniel said, finishing the difficult conversation.

Chapter 18
Phoebe and Isaiah and Dannie

Right Before Phoebe packed up and moved, her mother tried to persuade her to change her mind about going to live with Isaiah. She tried numerous tactics, from cajoling, flattering, and a sort of reasoning, to instructing, belittling, and even commanding her daughter, but none of these was effective.

"Thanks mom for your input. I will take it under consideration," was Phoebe's response to all of these tactics.

Phoebe arrived at the cabin with a few of her selected items in her car. A few other larger items that she treasured, such as a couple pieces of art work and a few pieces of furniture were to arrive shortly, as she had them shipped. She had put into storage whatever her renter didn't want in the house. Isaiah was there to greet her, and they must have hugged for at least five minutes before uttering any words.

Isaiah told her that he had put some lighting inside the den that he could control from his computer. This way he was able to get some daily videos of what the pups were up to before they emerged from the den, which would probably not be for another week or two.

The pups had grown about 3 times their initial size, and besides whimpering, were now even beginning to imitate a growl, and made attempts at some high pitched howling. Their eyes were open now and were blue, although they still could not see very well and bumped into each other frequently. They were no longer limited to sucking from Rebecca's teats, and had developed small milk incisors that enabled them to eat some pre-digested regurgitated meats. They even could stand up and move about a bit.

Isaiah showed off his recordings to Phoebe and she was thrilled with them. She felt that with what she already had that they were going to create a splendid wildlife documentary. She was going to give Isaiah a lot of the credit for the show once it aired. She would do the editing and be the narrator, but he was probably even more vital to this project.

Dannie and Abby arrived a couple of days after Phoebe had settled in. There was no real place for Dannie to stay in the cabin, but Phoebe offered to share their bed with them, and she accepted.

It was kind of late when they arrived. Abby of course went straight for Isaiah, and Isaiah let her bowl him over and lick his face, and any other exposed skin of his that she could find, as he hugged her and growled happy sounds to her. It was quite the scene, as the two women watched, laughing with gusto.

Dannie had brought a painting as a gift that she had created, inspired by Phoebe and Isaiah, from the short time they had spent together. It was not a large painting, but it was very colorful. It was of two vortexes of energy encircling each other, like a dance of two tornados. Phoebe thought it was magnificent, and said that she would hang it up by the head of their bed.

Meanwhile, Abby had let Isaiah up from his prone position on the floor. He also loved the painting of the two of them. He could tell that he was the slightly darker energy of purples and reds.

"Well, I had my greeting kiss. How about you two girls do the same," Isaiah said, deciding that he would get ahead of the inevitable, and get into control by his agreement.

"All right. That is a marvelous idea Isaiah," Dannie said. "I've been thinking of kissing you Phoebe, since that first moment we met," as she pulled Phoebe into her arms.

They started slowly sniffing each other's necks, then kissing them gently, as they both had their hair tied up in a kind of a bun on top of their heads. Phoebe had dark hair and Dannie was blond, both quite long. They used their hands to untie and loosen the buns and let the full heads of hair to flow down past their shoulders. They fondled each other's head, and stroked each other's long hair in a kind of synchronous action. This lovely feminine activity was starting to turn Isaiah on. He enjoyed the way they slowly kissed one another's necks with unhurried yet building passion. He felt that his own neck was being kissed and fondled.

The girls then put their hands behind the other one's head, pulling themselves closer, and began to kiss all over each other's face and hair, slowly approaching the lower center where their mouths sat. It seemed to Isaiah that there was a sexual struggle for control between the two women, to see who would be more of the sensual aggressor, and who would be the recipient of this affection. Being that Dannie was slightly taller and more experienced with women than Phoebe was, it looked to Isaiah that she was taking more control of the situation. Dannie was pushing Phoebe, who had her back toward the bed, in that direction. Both women were making wild sensual noises, soft moans to high pitched chirps that sounded like a dove taking off to fly. The sounds alone were a turn-on to Isaiah, as he closed his eyes for a minute to totally enrapt himself in this new sensual experience. The women were taking off each other's clothes, still moaning with every touch, while Isaiah had his eyes still closed. He opened both of his eyes, and saw the two women stark naked on the bed with their legs intertwined, with Dannie sort of on top and partly to the side of Phoebe.

Phoebe's head was partly off the edge of the bed, Dannie was sucking and kissing her breasts and in full control now, and Phoebe was getting off beautifully. Isaiah moved closer toward them and smelled their sexuality, exciting him further. Dannie was saying how wonderful Phoebe smelled and tasted, the best flavor in the world, as she started to move her head between Phoebe's legs. Isaiah whole heartedly agreed with her assessment.

Phoebe was persistently moaning, but between moans she told Isaiah to take off his clothes, and to put his cock in her mouth, as her head still hung over the side of the bed. Isaiah had never taken off his clothes as quickly, and inserted his engorged large penis gently into her mouth, standing at the side of the bed. She was very moist in her mouth as well as her pussy, which Dannie was having her way with. Phoebe could still make sounds, but she could no longer speak words, as she was being surrounded with pleasure from top to bottom.

The sight and physical presence of his member sliding slowly down and then back up from deep into her throat triggered an extra boost of energy that exploded from Phoebe's pussy for a number of thrusts, which Dannie could feel in her own genitals as well. After the initial boost, Isaiah could tell that the energy level had started to flatten off, and pulled his still but not quite as engorged penis from Phoebe's mouth. After a short break, Phoebe took hold of his cock with her left hand and pulled him closer to her. Her genital contractions started going back up, and she synchronously squeezed his penis with her hand encircling it, as if her hand were her pussy contracting around it, which felt totally amazing to Isaiah. They remained in this three ring revel for some time, when Phoebe let go of Isaiah's penis and stated that it was time for Dannie to get on her back and that she and Isaiah were going to gang up, and do her together. Isaiah turned Dannie over onto her back, as she protested, without any real intention to resist.

Phoebe told Isaiah to do Dannie's pussy with his hands and mouth if he so desired, and that she would perform on the breasts and face of Dannie. Isaiah stroked Dannie's long and well-developed thighs, especially the inner area, working his way toward her pussy. Phoebe stimulated Dannie's breasts, slowly and assuredly with both of her hands.

Dannie was moaning with desire, as the two lovers aggressed on her erotically. Isaiah placed the palm of his left hand on the area just above her clitoris and pulled and pressed on that area so that Dannie's clitoral hood was significantly drawn away from her clitoris, fully exposing it. Her clitoris was now uniquely revealed to his right hand fingers. He put a bit of lubricant on the tip of his index finger and proceeded to gently touch the inner sanctum of Dannie's upper left quadrant of her clitoris.

At about the same time, Phoebe put a bit of lubricant on her index finger tips and began to lightly touch and pleasure both of Dannie's nipples at the same speed and pressure that Isaiah was using on her clitoris. They were a fantastic team and were stroking and peaking Dannie as if they were one person with four hands. Dannie was squealing and moaning louder and louder, as the peaks were getting stronger and stronger. Dannie's clitoris was so engorged, and she was so wet. Her nipples were firm and pointing up. Isaiah no longer had to pull on her hood to expose her clitoris, which was now fully engorged, as were her nipples. Her contractions were constantly growing, and powerful. Again, at approximately the same time, Isaiah inserted his thumb easily into the opening of Dannie's vagina, as Phoebe inserted her tongue between the lips of Dannie's red mouth, as she kissed her full on with her own lips.

"You are our captive," Isaiah exclaimed, as they took Dannie up for one last giant peak that had the whole bed shake with the vibrations of her orgasm.

"Glory be, that was the best orgasm of my life," Dannie stated, as Phoebe and Isaiah kissed one another sitting over the prone blond. They took a short break and had some sweet red cherries that Dannie had brought with her to snack on.

"This has been a night of cherries for me," Phoebe affirmed.

"Me too," Isaiah repeated.

"We have not finished with you yet Mr. Phallus. You better get ready for us ganging up on you next," Dannie said, between bites of eating cherries.

"What do you think we should do to him Dannie, tie him up?" Phoebe asked in a sexy voice.

"How about we each get on opposite sides of him, as he lies down between us. I'll be on his left side since I am left handed, and you can be on his right side. We can each take one of his legs between both of our legs and kind of control his body with our legs. We can spread him apart and have our way with him and his erection, or kiss his ears, neck, mouth, and even his nipples if we so desire. Our hands will be free to manipulate whatever we desire," Dannie challenged in a racy and erogenous declaration.

"Wow, that sounds crazy divine. Okay Mr. Phallus, lie down right there and take it like a man," Phoebe commanded Isaiah with pure certainty.

Isaiah did as he was told. His member was pointing straight up, not to give away his preference, as the two women each put one of his legs between their thighs.

"Ahh, this already feels amazing. Your strong smooth legs are so sensual yet dominating at the same time," Isaiah proclaimed, ecstasy showing on his face, as Phoebe and Dannie squeezed and pulled apart his legs a little more, and began to kiss his neck and fondle his nipples.

Isaiah felt totally surrounded and in elation. Now Phoebe moved her thighs even higher toward his engorged penis and then Dannie did the same on her side. "My cock feels so good, so much attention, and you are not even touching it directly. This is so great," at which point Dannie moved her top leg so that her knee was bent and pointing toward the ceiling like his penis still was, and put her foot pressed up against his scrotal area.

Your leg bent like that Dannie looks so sexy," Phoebe remarked, as Dannie put some lubricant on her hand, and slowly applied it to Isaiah's very engorged penis.

Dannie then put her left hand around it, and started slowly stroking it up and down, and at the same time pressing her foot against his hidden cock under his scrotal area, while Phoebe got up on her hands and started kissing Isaiah on his mouth with her moist lips, and then adding her tongue to penetrate his lips, while Dannie played with his genitals. Isaiah was being ravished from so many angles, he felt entirely surrounded by this feminine sexual desire. Because of the love he felt from the way Phoebe was kissing him, and the fact that all he saw was Phoebe's face on top of his, it felt like Phoebe was kissing him and playing with his cock at the same time. He then realized that it was Dannie that was encircling his cock with her hands and feet, and even with her legs. Isaiah was on cloud 999.

Then Phoebe had another idea on how to use their legs to stimulate his penis, because Isaiah was so turned on by these sexy limbs, and also their feet. She put some lubricant on the bottom of her feet and sat at his side, while Dannie sat between his legs. Phoebe slipped his cock amid the souls of her smooth feet and started stroking his engorged staff with them, while Dannie was using her foot to stimulate his hidden cock.

"That feels so good. I love the way your calf muscles contract when you, ah ah, move your legs and feet up and down on me," Isaiah moaned and howled. An echoing howl emerged from the wilderness outside. Abby who was lying under the bed, perked up and howled back.

"I bet that's Barack and Rebecca adding their two cents in. They can tell that you are having a good time," Phoebe stated.

Isaiah was getting a secondary erection and was ready to explode, so the girls stopped at the same time, and then started stroking him again. They kept peaking him almost to squirting, as he was leaking seminal fluid over Phoebe and Dannie's feet. Phoebe's hand was pressing down and then releasing against his abdomen to add to the powerful sensations that he was having.

Dannie then started to hump his left leg with her crotch and press her knee against his hidden cock, while Phoebe switched over to her hands, up and down very slowly and deliberately over every square millimeter of his huge penis. Over and over she and Dannie repeated this onslaught, stopping each time just before he burst, then quickly taking him close to the edge again. Finally, Isaiah could not take any more, and the levee burst with a tremendous force that splashed them all with his ejaculate. Phoebe kept stroking his penis as long as he kept on coming and having sensation for the next couple of minutes, continually lightening up and slowing down on her stroke as his erection and orgasm were diminishing.

They all lay on their backs, listening to the wolves that were out hunting, howling in the distance. The three humans were sexually spent.

Isaiah finally spoke up, "I can't believe how high I went. The two of you together make a great team. I can still feel my body vibrating with sensation, and the energy that I felt when you both put your feet on my cock was like an atomic bomb going off. When you finally switched to your hands Phoebe, and you Dannie were riding my leg and pressing me so erotically with your knee, and I exploded like a supernova all over the place. It was so amazing. I will never forget it, no way."

"That was so much fun doing your phallus, Mr. Phallus," Dannie giggled and continued. "I was so well comed by the two of you earlier; it felt so natural to use my orgasm to spill over to yours. It was so much fun kissing you Phoebe, earlier, though that seems like many moons ago now, yet I can still feel my lips tingling upon your lips."

"Yes, that was the first erotic kiss with another woman for me, Dannie, and then your mouth on my pussy was so exotic and right on. It was so thrilling to have you, Isaiah, putting your member into my throat, so deeply, a new sensation. It was off the map for me, unexplored territory that was so thrilling and so orgasmic. I love or lust you both," Phoebe confessed.

"Well, you are a great kisser. It's hard to believe this was your first one with another woman," Dannie stated.

"Phoebe is a great kisser. I definitely agree with you on that," Isaiah responded.

Abby barked a couple of times.

"Yes, Abby, you are too," Isaiah added, as everyone laughed at their own happiness.

They were all spent after Isaiah had fixed them a wonderful tasty salad with some smoked salmon that he had cured himself, and his now famous sourdough bread. They all fell asleep rather quickly on the big bed, with Abby joining them at their feet.

Isaiah woke up first, and took Abby outside to relieve herself, and then created another gourmet meal of goat cheese and mushroom omelets with his sourdough sliced to toast. He had a bunch of different mushrooms that he had picked this past winter from the forest floor, and had dried and now rehydrated. He had gotten the cheese from a local goat farmer, and the eggs were also from a local farmer who raised chickens, so almost all the ingredients were local and fresh. The girls woke up to the fragrant odor of the food cooking on the *Wolf Range* stove that his mother had gifted him.

"Glory be, you should open up a restaurant. These are the best omelets I think I've ever eaten. They are even better than the *Olema Bistro*," Dannie exclaimed.

"It's true. Isaiah is a great cook, but he is such an outdoors person, I don't think a restaurant is in his future," Phoebe responded.

"Thank you for the compliment, Dannie, and the complement, Phoebe," Isaiah said, as he fed Abby some of his omelet, which she devoured with relish, licking her mouth numerous times with her tongue long after having swallowed the food.

"I've arranged for us to visit the sheep farm, where I met Stephanie last month, if you'd like," Isaiah offered, mostly to Phoebe but also to Dannie.

"Who is this Stephanie? She sounds formidable, the way you asked that question," Dannie asked.

"Oh, Isaiah met her a few weeks ago when his wolves devoured one of the sheep at this co-op ranch where Stephanie lives and works. He also had a fling with her at my urging. I have not met her yet, and that could be fun, as I did talk to her on the phone afterwards, and she seemed very nice, and yes, formidable," Phoebe answered.

Chapter 19
Aisha and Daniel

Stuff, so much stuff, material goods, possessions, just stuff, everywhere that Aisha went to. Aisha was in awe, or in shock from all the stuff on display in every market, and in every home that she visited. Aisha was becoming Americanized very quickly. She had never been in a large department store before. She thrilled at all the beautiful items available to those who had the money, and she loved the personal service and attention she received at *Bergdorf Goodman*. Bella helped her pick out a whole new wardrobe, and of course bought some items on her brother's dime for herself as well. Bella also took Aisha to a fancy hairdresser, where they gave her a new sexy style.

When Daniel told Aisha about Phoebe, she did not know what to think at first. She did not mind sharing a husband, but she wanted to be the number one wife. As far as she could tell, his first marriage had dissipated because of Daniel's supposed demise, which made her his only legitimate spouse.

Aisha came down to dinner that first night after buying her new clothes, wearing a very attractive fairly short red dress, and with her new hairdo, and looked like a super model. There was more than a bump in her abdomen where their babies were growing, but this only made her look more voluptuous.

"You look amazing dear. I have never seen you wear something that complimented your body before, as I have practically only seen you in your burqa. Your hair also looks fantastic. I have touched your skin under the covers, but the lights were always dim. I think I just won the lottery," Daniel stated, as he gazed upon her.

"I do like the way I look, though I am not sure that I like all the ogling and scrutiny that people were giving me at the stores when I tried the outfits on. It made me feel self conscious, but I guess I will have to get used to it. Besides, once the babies get bigger inside me, I won't look so glamorous," Aisha responded, as Bella and their parents also could not take their eyes off of her.

"I don't know about that. When Amy was pregnant with Daniel, she got even more beautiful," Saul Granger added.

Bella was a bit jealous. She had always been the apple of her father's eyes, her daddy's girl, and here was this new woman taking much of his attention from her. Phoebe was also very beautiful, but her dad had never looked at her the way he noticed Aisha.

"Thanks for the compliment dear. I did look good when I was carrying Daniel. Not so much when I was with Bella, but I was already quite a bit older by then," Amy chimed in.

"You always look great my dear Amy, and once Bella was delivered, you regained your shape in no time. I think Aisha kind of looks like you too," Saul added, much to Bella's chagrin.

This lack of attention infuriated Bella. She decided to get even with Aisha, even though Aisha really had not done anything to her. On the next day, Bella anonymously reported to *Homeland Security* that she overheard this woman in a store talking on her cell phone with people that were planning to bomb the *Statue of Liberty,* and gave them enough information so that they could figure out who she was referring to.

Two days later, after the false informant call, the FBI came to their home and arrested Aisha. Daniel was already on his way to the city when his dad called him to tell him what had occurred. Bella had already returned to California by then, and had actually forgotten the mischief that she had perpetrated, thinking that nothing would amount from her call.

Daniel called his newsroom to find out more information. They did not know anything at the time, being that it just happened, so he called a friend he knew at the FBI. His friend told him that they arrested his wife, on a citizen's tip, and were questioning her. Daniel found out where they were detaining her, and called one of the lawyers for *ABC* to meet him there.

Aisha was frightened. She did not want to be sent back to Afghanistan. She cooperated as best as she could, denying all accusations that they hurled at her. The agents asking the questions were thorough and tried to get her to admit her potential crimes, and with who else she was working with. Aisha had of course no idea what they were talking about. Daniel and his lawyer got to the detention center, and they allowed the lawyer to speak with Aisha. He told her not to answer any more questions, until he finished talking with her, and the agents had to wait outside while he found out what was going on.

Meanwhile, someone from the local New York City *CBS News* station had been doing an expose story about the detention center, and were privy to the account of Aisha's arrest and detention. They put the story out as a news release that was picked up by all the major news agencies and wires. The story was becoming bigger, and was already being spread as breaking news throughout the country. Daniel of course preferred that this story would just disappear, but he knew that he had to fight back against these false incriminations against his wife. They kept her overnight at the center in a holding cell, and she was arraigned the next day for trial. Because she was so attractive with a baby inside her, she did not fit the terrorist profile. The judge let her out on bail, and also Daniel's recognizance. Daniel vouched for his wife and gladly paid the bail. Daniel was just happy that they did not send her to *Guantanamo*, or back to Afghanistan.

"I don't understand this country. I have not done anything wrong, yet I am being punished just for being a Muslim," Aisha cried, though feeling relief for being allowed to leave the jail. Daniel tried to comfort her outside the courthouse. Reporters were flocking around them like gulls to a beached fish.

"We have a great lawyer, and hopefully this will blow over quickly, and we can get all the charges dropped. The United States government here has been overzealous after the World Trade Center bombings, and I guess they would rather be safe than sorry, but this is really ridiculous. I don't know who could have done this to you. I guess I may have made some enemies in covering stories here and abroad. Perhaps even the Taliban could be behind this. We will probably never know," Daniel said, holding his wife close to him, trying to comfort her, to some success.

Chapter 20
Phoebe Isaiah Dannie and Stephanie

"This is awful news. They just arrested Daniel's wife Aisha for being a potential terrorist. They let her out on bail, as they had no real proof, but this will do damage to his well being, and to his image, not to mention her freedom," Phoebe said to both Isaiah and Dannie, as they were driving to the sheep farm.

"Is there anything that we can do?" Isaiah asked.

"Not much, though we can call Daniel, and let him know that we are all pulling for them, just let him know that we care. There is probably nothing anyone can do, except for a good lawyer, and they probably have one of those already," Phoebe responded.

"If she is innocent, then I'm sure that they will dismiss the case quickly. They can't just jail someone who is blameless. Can they?" Dannie asked.

"I like your attitude Dannie," Isaiah responded, "but they can do whatever the hell they want. Hopefully, it will all go away quickly, but with these kind of charges, they have a lot of leeway, even deporting her back to Afghanistan or Guantanamo."

"We don't want that," Phoebe added, feeling a bit guilty for thinking about her own desires and relationships, when she was miles away from the problem.

"I love these back roads and driving through these hilly woods," Dannie stated, taking out a joint, lighting it, and passing it around in order to change the somber mood to one being more festive.

"I haven't smoked any pot in a long time," both Isaiah and Phoebe responded simultaneously.

They each took a toke nonetheless, and felt very stoned almost immediately.

"I used to smoke quite a bit in college. I was quite good at driving and smoking, actually made me drive slower, but I would miss exits more often when stoned," Isaiah said.

"I still smoke or do edibles all the time. I'm glad that it is legal now and so easy to get, even though it was never really hard to find. It makes me feel more creative, and lets me paint with more freedom. I will take some photos with my phone of all the beauty around here, and perhaps use these scenes in a painting or two," Dannie remarked.

"That gives me an idea," Phoebe added. "I can take some video recordings of the sheep farm, and maybe include it in our wolf documentary, or in a separate documentary, if *National Geographic* would prefer that."

Isaiah got them to the farm with no problems, even though his driving slowed down along with their clocks. Stephanie was there to greet them when they got out of Daniel's truck. Being that they were all quite stoned, they gave Stephanie huge hugs before even being introduced by Isaiah. Phoebe gave Stephanie a kiss, saying that she was rewarding her for past good behavior. Stephanie could smell the pot on their clothes and on Phoebe's breath.

"It's nice to meet you too Phoebe, and you as well, Dannie," Stephanie said, after the introductions. "I like pot too, but I have to tell you that you guys reek of it. Maybe I will do an edible to be on the same plane as you. The only problem with the edibles is that it takes so long for me to feel the effects. However, it's better than smoking it for me, as smoking always dries my throat out too much."

"Yes, it does. Do you have some water bottles available? I can definitely use a drink," Phoebe said, as Stephanie brought them 3 large reusable bottles of spring water.

"It looks like all the sheep are sheared. They look so different without their coats on, much smaller," Isaiah said, looking around.

"We have the last batch of sheep being sheared right now. Would you like to see the process?" Stephanie asked.

"That would be so cool," Dannie responded, as Phoebe and Isaiah both agreed.

Stephanie led them into a large barn. There was a couple guys handling the sheep.

"We tried using this robot shearer at our last place, which was invented in Australia, but we like the results with using human hands and electric shears better here," Stephanie said.

One of the shearers, a big fellow, was holding the sheep while the other was using the electric shearing clippers. It seemed to go real quickly. There was a motor for the shears that made a ratchet noise on the ceiling, and the fleecing of the sheep went quickly and smoothly.

"It only takes a couple of minutes to shear a whole sheep, if one knows what they are doing. We try to keep them as clean as possible beforehand, no hay to eat or sleep on, actually no food for about a week, so that there will be less feces and debris on the sheared off wool. We really want them as clean as possible. We do what is called crutching in late autumn, where we remove the fleece around their anal area, so that it stays cleaner and drier, and they don't get blow flies that can cause flystrike, which can kill them. We also do wigging at the same time to remove the fleece from around their eyes so that they are able to see."

Stephanie continued with her lesson. "After shearing we do what is called skirting. Skirting is where we put the sheared fleece on a large table, the outside facing up, and remove with our hands any excess crud that is on the fleece. We then wash the skirted fleece. We also remove the part that was around the sheep's butt and belly, because those areas are dirtier and less esteemed. We also pick out any grass or burrs that are stuck on the fleece," Stephanie informed her guests.

"How do you wash the fleece after you skirt it?" Phoebe asked, recording the event with both video and sound.

"We put the fleeces in large compacted bales and fork lift them to the next building. We then have to wash the fleece in special hot soapy water a few times to remove all the grime and the lanolin or wool grease out of them. Then it has to go through numerous rinses until the rinse water is clear. The washing process is known as scouring. We then dry the fleeces in drying machines or on large racks to air dry. The washing, drying, picking, and carding machines, where we straighten out the fibers of the wool are in the large building next door. After washing the fleece, we remove the lanolin from the wash water, which we sell to cosmetic companies that use it for hand and body lotions," Stephanie informed her audience.

Stephanie continued her lecture tour, taking them to the next building. "We use well water that we recycle, plus we have built a water collecting system to catch the rain water in the winter rainy season. We use only a special detergent that is biodegradable and compostable. We can also compost any parts of the fleece that we are unable to use. We have solar panels that you saw as you came in, to produce the electricity to run all these machines. We even create extra electricity that we can sell back to PG&E."

"That is all so impressive. And you spin and dye the wool into yarn here too?" Isaiah asked, while Abby ran outside the building, only Isaiah noticing.

"Yes, but we dye and make finished products in another smaller building. We have a couple looms that we can use to weave sweaters and clothing, and a couple of the women here like to knit, but most of the yarn we sell as is. But first, after washing and drying we take the fleece and put it into that machine over there called the picking machine that blows it into that room next to it. It separates the wool into smaller pieces, teasing or picking it apart, opening the locks, and blows it around, kind of fluffing it up. One can add spinning oil that helps the fibers slide against each other and helps them stick together in a fine web. One can also add other natural or manmade fibers in the picking room to create a wool blend, but we usually only make pure wool yarn here. After picking, the wool has to be carded and combed, which are those two large machines that are over there, which straightens out the fibers into long unidirectional strands that are called first, wool webs, and finally into pencil rovings. The carding and combing also removes any knots and debris that was left after washing and picking."

Stephanie continued with the tour and lecture. "The wool rovings looks like yarn but are easily pulled apart until it is spun on the spinner over there, which puts the actual twist on the yarn. We use large machines here, but remember those fairy tales with the girls and Rumplestilskin using a spinning wheel. The term spinster was derived from women who would spin wool and other yarns on a spinning wheel, and later became synonymous with an unmarried woman. The rovings are only held together by the oil and natural hooks on the surface of the wool fibers. We can then spin it on spinning jennys without breaking those fibers. The spun fibers are put onto wooden bobbins. Single ply yarn is still not very strong. One can twist two strands together from two bobbins on a plyer to get double ply, and even greater ply if you prefer. Finally the yarn on the bobbin is transferred to paper cones on a cone winder to use on weaving and knitting machines, or into skeins of yarn for knitters to use," Stephanie related.

"Where is Abby?" Dannie asked.

"She went outside when we came in here," Isaiah answered. "Do you want me to get her?"

"She is probably with Mike, our 'sheep' dog, or actually our Border Collie. He is a good sort and probably showing her around," Stephanie said.

"As long as she is all right, we can get her later," Dannie said, feeling relieved.

"At what point do you dye the wool?" Phoebe asked, changing the topic back to the wool from doggerel.

"You can actually do that at anytime, but we like to do that at the end of the process here. We sell a lot of our wool undyed to manufacturers, but we do occasional dying here as well, with natural dyes that are biodegradable of course," Stephanie answered.

They all went back outside. Abby came running to greet them, first to Isaiah and then to Dannie. Mike followed Abby, and also went up to sniff Isaiah.

"Dogs really like you, don't they?" Stephanie asked rhetorically.

"That is an understatement," Phoebe responded anyway. "Isaiah is the pied piper of dogs, wolves, and all the Canines or Canidae, as far as I can tell, though I have not seen him around foxes or coyotes yet."

"I don't know, you seem pretty foxy to me Phoebe, and so does Dannie for that matter," Stephanie teased, as Dannie and Phoebe both giggled.

"I have a question Stephanie. Is it better to birth a lamb before or after shearing?" Isaiah asked, changing the subject off of him and his foxy friends.

"We like to shear the ewes first, but it depends on the climate, and the specific farm, and also the kind of sheep. We have a number of ewes giving birth already, and in the next month all the lambs should be born. Ewes go into heat usually in September through December, so we like to wait toward the end or their breeding season to introduce the rams to fertilize them. There is about a five month gestation period. This way we get to shear them in early to mid spring and they give birth at the end of spring, in late April, and in May. It's easier and cleaner for the lambs to suckle, without all that wool," Stephanie answered, "plus once they give birth it's best not to shear them for a couple weeks at least, as some of their veins are more protruding and you want them fully fed when lactating."

"So you separate the rams from the ewes the rest of the time then?" Phoebe asked.

"Well, we castrate a lot of the male lambs a couple weeks after they are born. At first we keep the uncastrated male lambs together with the ewes, but have to separate them when they get old enough to do it, which is after they are about 6 months old, which is usually in the fall for us. The castrated lambs can graze and hang with the rest of the ewes."

"Now I'll take you to the barn where there are some of the mothers with the new born lambs," Stephanie went on, and they all followed her, including Mike and Abby.

"Wow, this baby lamb is so cute. She is already walking. How old do you think it is?" Phoebe asked, still recording the goings-on.

"That one there is about a day old. They start walking almost right away, so they can reach their mother's teats. The first milk or colostrum is very important for a healthy lamb. The ewe mother will lick off the birthing wetness from the lamb's coat so that they will be drier. Otherwise they would get too chilly with our cool nights here, and could get sick. Most births are single ones, but we do get quite a few twins, and an occasional triplet birth, especially with the ewes that are between 3 and 6 years of age. The yearlings usually only have one lamb if any," Stephanie answered.

"Are the twins fraternal twins or are they identical?" Dannie asked, noticing a ewe with two babies that looked very much alike.

"I'm told that about 99% of the twins are fraternal, but that pair there that you are looking at are probably identical. They look so much alike. We have not done a

DNA test yet, and probably don't have to," Stephanie responded, taking them over to the three day old twins and letting them pet the cute critters. "We also have occasional interns, and some of the member's children staying in here, and petting the lambs frequently, so that they will get some human imprinting, and be easier to control later on. We keep them, the lambs that is, in the barn for about 5 days, and then let them outside to join the rest of the herd, so they can start eating a little bit of grass. They stay by their mother's side for about 4 months, at which time they are weaned."

"This is all so interesting, even if I wasn't stoned," Isaiah said.

"I find it fascinating as well," Phoebe exclaimed.

"How many dogs do you have on hand to herd the sheep here?" Isaiah asked.

"We've got about 500 sheep and we have 3 dogs, Mike, Daphne, and Herminie. We have electronic fences around the grazing area, but your wolves must have snuck in by the watering hole. We plan to carry about a thousand sheep maximum, and to sell the excess to other ranchers and people who want to have a sheep as a pet, or to start their own herd. Once we get more sheep we will probably get one or two more dogs. Maybe Abby will want to apply for the job," Stephanie joked.

"Ha ha, very funny. Abby and I live by the ocean in Marin, and even though Mike and Isaiah live up here, I am going to keep her with me." Dannie said, somewhat defensively.

"All of a sudden, I'm really hungry. I guess I have the munchies," Phoebe said.

"And you are eating for two now, possibly more," Isaiah reminded her.

"Zowie, you didn't tell me. Congratulations, but I'm not surprised either. I wouldn't mind eating either, and it's just for one," Dannie said.

"Why don't you take your foxes to that restaurant that I took you to Isaiah? It's really the only good place around here. I've got some work to do and I'm not really hungry, as I ate lunch early today," Stephanie said, and then offered. "When you come back, maybe we can have some more fun together. You can leave Abby here with Mike until you get back."

"I can live with that," Dannie responded.

Under Daniel's personal supervision, Aisha was allowed to stay in America. Aisha's phone records were checked by NSA, and there was nothing incriminating on it Through his friends in the government and in the FBI, plus a good lawyer from *ABC*, Daniel was able to get Aisha cleared of all charges. Paparazzi were still bothering them, so he decided to call Phoebe and see if they could hide out in some *Airbnb* somewhere nearby where she lived. He really wanted to see her and for her to meet Aisha, who wanted to meet Phoebe as well, and to get the hell out of Dodge for now. Daniel also had a strange desire to meet this Isaiah fellow.

While having lunch and having their munchies satisfied with good eats, Phoebe remembered that she wanted to call Daniel to offer her support.

She speed dialed Daniel who was calling her at the exact same time. Neither phone rang, but they both said hello, and thought *this is kind of weird*.

"Hi Daniel, I was calling you because I heard about what happened with Aisha, and wanted to offer my sympathy and support," Phoebe began.

"That's so very kind of you Phoebe, I was actually calling you just now to see if you can help us out. My parent's home is being swarmed by Paparazzi because of the incident. My folks are not happy about it, and Aisha is afraid to go out when they are all there with their cameras out front. The good news is that we got the government to drop all charges, so she is no longer a suspect. We need to escape from this place. I was hoping maybe that we could come see you and hang out for a while, maybe a couple of weeks or so, in a nice *Airbnb* close to where you and Isaiah are."

"Isaiah is right here, so I am going to tell him what you want and see if that is okay with him. I'll call you back in a couple minutes Daniel."

Isaiah answered before Phoebe even asked him the question. "Yes, we have to help them out. I know someone in town, it's not too close, but close enough. She could probably rent them out a nice home for a month."

"That would be great, I think. Aisha is starting her third trimester, so they will want to be closer to civilization fairly soon," Phoebe said, as she redialed Daniel.

"Isaiah is on board 100%. He even knows a possible place that you can stay. It may not be up to your standards of Scarsdale, but it probably beats your Afghan residences," Phoebe related.

"Perfect, it won't be forever. I want to get Aisha near a great hospital before she delivers. There is a fine hospital in Aurora, Colorado, only 17 miles from Denver. It's near mountains, so Aisha should feel at home too. It's also near the airport, so I will be able to travel for my work. I know some folks there who can help us find a place too. Another benefit, there shouldn't be too many Paparazzi around. I think the clamor will die down soon anyhow. Stories these days only last for a day to a week and then everyone moves on to the next story and forgets the last big one," Daniel responded.

"So when will you come here then?" Phoebe asked.

"I'll book a flight today and rent a car when we get there. Would tomorrow or the day after be okay? What is the closest airport?" Daniel asked.

Isaiah took the phone. "Your best bet is to fly into Redding. You can get a flight to SFO, or Oakland, or

Sacramento, or even Medford, Oregon, and then get a second flight to Redding, or to drive directly. We are about 75 miles east of Redding. I'll text you the address and phone number of the *Airbnb* where you can probably stay. I'll make arrangements as soon as I get off the phone, and contact my friends."

"Thanks, I really appreciate that. I look forward to meeting you soon. We might spend a day or two in San Francisco first," Daniel related.

"I hope that I've done the right thing," Phoebe said, after they got off the phone with Daniel.

"I think you responded perfectly, Phoebe. When a friend or family asks for help, we have to say yes at first. If it feels like something is wrong, or you are being taken advantage of, and it starts feeling awkward, or that you are doing something that you don't want to do, then you can always change your yes to something less, but until then, yes is the correct answer," Isaiah responded with one long breath.

"What do you think about Stephanie's offer of fun?" Dannie asked.

"I really like her. She is really sensual and friendly. We can go back there and see what kind of fun she wants to do. I'm game. What about you Dannie?" Phoebe answered and asked.

"Well, you know her better than me. I'll have to see what she wants to do, but I'm not against having fun, that's for sure," Dannie responded.

"I guess you feel you don't have to ask me, and you are right," Isaiah jested.

The meal was finally delivered and they ate with total enthusiasm.

They got back to the ranch, and Stephanie greeted them with a big smile on her face. She handed each of them another water bottle and a bath towel. "There is this hot springs and a lake nearby that we are going to go to first, if you would like." She also gave them some edibles to recharge their stoniness.

"The lake water is really deep here. It's fed by a hot geyser and a nearby fresh cold spring also. The top layer is warm. But if you dive down deeper, you will find it much cooler. Being that it is pre-summer, I suggest that you stay on top," Stephanie reported.

They all took off their clothes and first got into the hot mineral spring water that flowed into and out of a large stone formation before it mixed into the lake. There was a natural edge where one could even sit down. The girls were giggling because Isaiah was having a bit of a stone formation too.

"Maybe you should go into the cold water first Isaiah," Dannie joked.

"I'm not going to wield it like a battle axe. There is no need to worry," Isaiah responded in good humor.

"Which one of us is responsible for his condition?" Phoebe asked.

"We can do a test and see which way it points when we move around him," Dannie suggested.

"Okay, okay, I admit it. It was me. I was remembering the fun time I had with Isaiah the last time he was here with me, and seeing him naked triggered my memory," Stephanie related with a huge grin on her face, as if she had swallowed the proverbial canary.

"I thought it was me. I too was having my memory triggered from last night when I was playing with Phoebe and Isaiah," Dannie said.

"That makes three of us. I too was having sexual thoughts about Isaiah and about what the three of us can do to him," Phoebe related.

The girls giggled some more after talking about their lustful thoughts.

"Well, I guess we don't need to do the test then. We are all guilty of this carnal sin. So Phoebe what ideas did you come up with," Dannie requested.

"I thought we could start by having him lying down on the bed with us all around him and then getting like a minute to play with his toy each, and then passing the baton on to the next player. While we wait for our turn, we can watch the active agent pleasuring Isaiah, and also be self pleasuring our own pussys at the same time. At some point we can take turns by sitting over his face and letting him lick our pussy, still facing the girl who is doing him," Phoebe suggested.

"That is a great idea Phoebe. I think we can add our legs and feet into touching his toy too, knowing how turned on he gets just thinking about that," Dannie proposed.

"I think you are right, I am going to go into the cooler lake now. I'm already getting too turned on here," Isaiah remarked, as he got up. Before he could jump into the lake, the naked Phoebe, with her dark hair, grabbed him in an embrace and rubbed her body against his.

"Come over here you two," Phoebe called to her female friends, as she turned her back on Isaiah and rubbed her butt against his firmness.

Stephanie the redhead and Danni the blond took the left and right arms of Isaiah respectively, and tenderly pushed him back down in his original sitting position. The women then took turns giving him a small dose of what was promised, with a lap dance with their naked bodies upon his naked body, to the sound of the water lapping over the edge of the pool.

The women were howling like wolves in heat, and Isaiah was awash with ecstasy, howling right back at them. This erotic dance did not last all that long, but it gave Isaiah notice that he would be their plaything that day, and that he was going to have to surrender to his pleasure and theirs. He was up for that, at least presently.

"Okay," Phoebe announced. "Its time to go swimming," as they all got up and jumped into the cool waters. This tempered their heat, yet the new sensation on their bodies felt extremely sensual and invigorating. Phoebe swam over to Isaiah and lavished a big kiss on his mouth. She could feel his lips all over her body, in her mind, and in his.

They spent about another thirty minutes swimming and frolicking in the clear waters, occasionally immersing themselves in the hot pool when they got too chilled in the cold lake.

"We can all go back to my room and finish what we started," Stephanie remarked, with a twinkle in her eyes.

Dannie stated, "Why don't we rent out a room at the inn, one with a big king size bed? That way we will have more room to move about and have more privacy. Isaiah told us that you have a nice room Stephanie, but that it was fairly small, especially with a number of folks milling around. I will pay for it too, and this way we won't dirty all your towels and bedding."

"Gosh, that's a nice offer. It's true about my room. I think that's a great idea," Stephanie responded.

"Great idea Dannie," Phoebe and Isaiah said at the same time, agreeing with the assessment.

Isaiah and Dannie went to the front desk of the inn and rented out the honeymoon suite, their largest room available for the day, with Dannie's credit card. Phoebe and Stephanie joined them shortly thereafter, after purchasing some goodies, some lubricant, plus condoms at the pharmacy, just in case they wanted to.

It's a nice room. They all are inside and lock the door. It's quiet, but Dannie has her *IPhone*, and puts on her favorite *Pandora* station. They all are still quite high from the edibles. Phoebe takes off her top, exposing her sexy breasts. The other girls do the same.

They gang up on Isaiah and rip off his shoes and his pants without using words, but letting out quiet howls at first, exposing his once again stiff phallus.

Isaiah is howling back at the 3 women. He feels powerful, yet a victim of pleasure. He knows any resistance is futile, and surrenders and lets them push him onto the bed. The girls surround him like Phoebe suggested. They first slide their hands sensually all over his body at the same time, everywhere except his mast, which is standing tall in the center. They take turns kissing his lips. He is getting more and more excited. The women are too, and the howls are building.

Dannie goes first and coats his mast with some of the lubricant. Phoebe and Stephanie are watching closely and putting lubricant on their own pussys at the same time. Dannie starts stroking with her hands and using her left foot under his scrotum to have Isaiah again feel surrounded by her.

"Wow, that feels so amazing. It feels like you are doing me with your pussy, Dannie. This room also has a distinct fragrant pussy sexual odor," Isaiah says, as he takes a couple of deep breaths.

Dannie still takes Isaiah up and up, higher and higher, at one point, at the highest point, he is howling with delight as the sensation blasts every cell in his fully erect penis, and quickly spreads to his head, so he sees bright stars exploding with passion in his personal universe, even though his eyes are closed. Dannie peaks him at this height, stops her onslaught, and releases him from her control; passing the baton to the next sexy man tamer, who is Stephanie, and allowing Isaiah to come back to earth.

"It was so nice to finally get to kiss you. Forbidden fruit always tastes best. Your cock is amazing too. I am now going to take you up again using my two naked feet on either side of your shaft," Stephanie said, spreading her legs out with her feet together, which also exposes her pussy to Isaiah.

As soon as she puts her smooth, lubricant coated, cool feet upon his penis, Isaiah gave out a huge howl.

"That is oh, oh, oh, wowzee, so slick, ah ah, so sensssaaaayyytional Stephanie," Isaiah moaned, as pre-ejaculate fluid appeared at the tip of his penis, while the redhead gracefully continued her consistent rhythmic onslaught on him with the bottom of her feet, using both her arches and all ten toes.

"I'm going to lick that off the tip of your penis, Isaiah. Don't stop Steph. Keep stroking just like you are doing girl. You got him so good there. He is so high and in total bliss," Phoebe stated, as she licked off the precum, which just reappeared as soon as she licked off the top level; then giving the crown of his cock a couple extra swirls with her tongue.

Meanwhile Dannie was self pleasuring and really getting into it. "Give me a few licks too, will you Phoebe, please," she requested.

As soon as Phoebe finished licking Isaiah, she came right over to the beautiful natural blond with the blond pubic hair, and pushed her flat on the bed and started some girl on girl cunnilingus.

"You get an extra turn on that big toy. It's such a turn-on watching you control it with your sexy feet," Dannie spoke, and yelping at the same time from Phoebe's tongue.

Stephanie decided to switch positions. She seized his engorged throbbing cock with her hands and put her left knee alongside and under his scrotum. The redhead was pressing and releasing her knee against his hidden cock at the same time she stroked his visible firm cock with her hands.

"You've got such a great cock Isaiah. It is so responsive to whatever I do to you. I totally feel it in my pussy too," Stephanie exhorted.

The pleasure yowling and moaning of both Dannie and Isaiah was mounting, as if they were somehow feeling the same pleasures.

"You are superbly superb at licking my pussy," Dannie said between yelps.

Isaiah was totally overpowered by Stephanie's sexual desire for his cock and had surrendered totally to each and every one of her erotic actions.

"I can feel so much. It is so intense. You got me so good Stephanie. It feels like your feet and your hands are controlled by your pussy. They have me, ah ah. It smells so sexy in here, so electric, high voltage. That stroke, right there, just now, so tremendous, ah, ah, completely under your sexual supremacy," Isaiah wailed.

Then the foursome switched partners. Dannie sucked and licked on Stephanie's pussy, rewarding her for such a splendid job on Isaiah, and Isaiah was allowed to use his hands and also lick on Phoebe's delicious pussy. Now the moans were coming from Stephanie and Phoebe in a crescendo path, as both their genitals were contracting simultaneously. The room was getting really hot.

"You taste insanely good," Isaiah said between licks, his penis still engorged and ready for more action too.

Stephanie asked Dannie to lower the temperature on the Air Conditioner, and said she wanted to lick Phoebe's insanely tasty pussy next. Dannie got back on the bed and took hold of Isaiah's long rod, as Stephanie went down on Phoebe.

Dannie switched very quickly to using a very light stroke on Isaiah's shaft, as he was close to bursting as soon as she started her rhythmic assault. At this point he was totally surrendered to pussy power, and anything Dannie did brought him close to exploding. She started a light tapping motion up and down his penis, which drove him sexually crazy; loud moans and wolf howls emanating from deep in his throat. She had to slow down her tapping or he would burst from this sexually simple engagement. Phoebe joined him in a chorus of howling moans that filled the room. She was having strong contractions from Stephanie's physical manipulations with her mouth and hands on her clitoris and labia.

"You have the best tasting pussy that I ever had Phoebe," Stephanie said, licking her own lips, as she lifted her head up for air, continuing to maneuver upon Phoebe's clitoris and vaginal opening with her fingers. Phoebe was moaning with even more gusto, as Stephanie put her fingers inside Phoebe's wet and desirous vagina, massaging where the G-spot was alleged to be found.

Phoebe was moaning even louder. Stephanie obviously found some erotic spot, as Phoebe's moans were triggering Isaiah's carnal responses. At this point, Dannie got in a position where she could stroke Isaiah's penis with her foot, with her calf muscle flexing below her bent knee. She was stroking with her hands at the same time. This was just too much for Isaiah, as he gave one tremendous thunderous wail followed by decreasing howls, as the dam burst open, flooding over Dannie's body, and upon the bedding with oodles of his sexual seed.

Phoebe was synchronized with her beloved Isaiah, and had a final intense climax. Stephanie slowly brought her down with some firmer pressure, as Isaiah was releasing his load, to becoming a less intense level of being.

"Zowie, that was so much fun," Dannie stated, as she milked the last drops of fluid from Isaiah's penis.

"You girls have overwhelmed me with all your limbs and pussy juices. I have never been so sexually high ever. When you added your foot back in Dannie, your sexy calf muscle shining with sexuality, and Phoebe was grunting like a wild animal over there, I just couldn't take it any longer, and I exploded with such immensely powerful sensations. It felt like I may never come down from there," Isaiah said, after he got his breath back.

"Yes, Phoebe was a wild woman there. It was so much fun licking and doing her. I loved how she tasted, as you know. I am so glad we did this here. If it was in my room, my neighbors would have freaked out," Stephanie concurred.

"I loved how we kept changing partners. Each time was unique and it kept on building higher in this room, till Isaiah and I exploded separately, yet together," Phoebe exclaimed.

They exchanged a few more frames. "It was so sexy when you spread your legs and massaged my penis with your two feet and flashed me with your pussy and your red pubic hair, Stephanie," Isaiah moaned again, just thinking about it.

"It was so sweet when Phoebe licked your penis while I was doing that," Stephanie added.

After the romp in the hotel room, they drove back to the ranch, picked up Abby, who was still with Mike, but came running over to the truck, as soon as they pulled up, to greet Isaiah, and Dannie as well. The three travelers gave Stephanie big hugs and thanks for an amazing day, and drove back to the cabin.

"That redheaded woman is even more uninhibited than me. I really enjoyed her promiscuity and energy. You are the man Isaiah, and a very lucky man to have found Phoebe. And Phoebe you made this all happen, so generous and sexy, and lucky to have found Isaiah. Thank you from the bottom of my pussy. This was one of the best days of my life," Dannie said affectionately on the ride back.

"Thank you, you are so kind to say that. I don't know about luck, but I do feel extremely fortunate for having met Isaiah. I think your fun loving energy Dannie was responsible for a lot of what transpired. We wouldn't have done it without you and your desires," Phoebe responded.

By the time they got back to the cabin, they had come down from the drugs they had ingested and all were tired and hungry. Isaiah microwaved some leftover vegetables. They voraciously ate them up along with some sweet potato chips that Isaiah had previously concocted. The three adventurers all went to bed and slept real soundly.

Chapter 21
Aisha Daniel Phoebe Isaiah

Uneventfully, except for some Paparazzi hanging by his parent's home, Daniel and Aisha left the next day for the West coast. He decided that he would show Aisha San Francisco for a couple of days first, staying at the *St. Regis Hotel,* and then drive up to see Phoebe and her new guy. He called Bella to tell her of his plans, and if she wanted to meet them at the *Embarcadero* for a late lunch that day or the next day. Bella was acting quite weird, Daniel thought, and had made up an excuse of having to study for an exam, which seemed strange to him. She never in his recollection would choose studying over anything else. Perhaps, he thought, she was growing up, and becoming more diligent.

Bella felt so guilty hearing her beloved brother's voice that she called Phoebe afterwards to confess her crimes.

"Oh man, that is horrendous," was Phoebe's initial response. Phoebe then said, "I think you've got to tell him what you just told me. He will be upset at first, but he will eventually forgive you, knowing Daniel. You sound awful, and having that load on your conscience will keep you stuck and miserable for a long time. You acted out of envy, and you can say to him how you know it was a stupid thing to do. You didn't think there would be such big repercussions, and you are so very sorry for having acted vindictively. Tell him that you really like Aisha, and think she is especially beautiful, and that you want to make it up to them, and ask for his forgiveness, even beg him for his forgiveness. He may get very angry at you at first, but he will come around. I know him well."

Bella started sobbing over the phone. "You are right as usual Phoebes, sob sob. I will call him back. I have not slept well since I did that, sob sob. Please don't tell him right away, in case I get cold feet again, sob sob."

"Listen Bella, no cold feet. You have to tell him a.s.a.p. It is for your own sanity. Listen, I'm going to hang up now, so you can call your brother immediately. Good bye," Phoebe implored.

Bella's feet were still kind of cold, but she texted her brother what Phoebe had suggested, instead of speaking with him directly, which would have been the appropriate thing to do, but at least she got it off her chest. Her feet felt surprisingly warmer afterwards.

Daniel was devastated. His own sister had betrayed him and Aisha. Presently, he felt like he never wanted to see or speak with her again. He told Aisha, and she was not as angry as he was.

"We must forgive her Daniel. She is just a young silly girl who made a foolish mistake out of jealousy. At least she told you, and she did ask you for forgiveness. Allah is known as being compassionate and merciful. Our beloved prophet Mohammed said that whoever suffers an injury and forgives the perpetrator of that attack, that Allah will raise their status to a higher level, and remove one of their sins. I know I wouldn't mind having any one of my sins removed," Aisha said, poking Daniel, and then kissing him.

"You are a better person than me Gunga Din. I still feel angry toward that brat. She could have at least called me, or told me to my face, instead of an obnoxious text message, but you are right. Anger is most harmful to the one who is angry, so I am going to give it up too, and become more like you. I wouldn't mind my status being elevated either. See, I feel better already thanks to you," Daniel said, kissing his beloved.

"Thanks dear Daniel, but who is this Gunga Din?" Aisha asked.

"Oh, I'm sorry. He was a character in a famous poem by Rudyard Kipling, a British writer living in India. The last line of the poem is, Y*ou're a better man than I am, Gunga Din,"* Daniel responded, kissing Aisha on her forehead.

Daniel showed Aisha some of the key sights in San Francisco. They walked to the *Embarcadero,* where they had a late lunch at the *Waterbar Restaurant.* Aisha loved the view of the bay and the *Bay Bridge.* She had never seen an aquarium like these before, especially strange for the large tanks being in a restaurant. They ate some of the best oysters that even Daniel had ever eaten. The sky was a bright blue, about 70 degrees, a delightful day to see San Francisco. After lunch they walked from the *Embarcadero* to *Fisherman's Wharf.* The wharf was a bit too touristy, but Aisha enjoyed seeing all the sea lions laying about.

Daniel called Phoebe after getting back to the hotel. "I found out who called Homeland Security. It was Bella of all people. Aisha is such a good person, and wants me to forgive her, as she has already."

"At least she had the gumption to call you and admit her faux pas," Phoebe responded.

"That is putting it euphemistically, I'd say, and she didn't call, she texted me, so I have not even spoken to her yet. Aisha and I had a nice afternoon by the bay, and ate the best oysters I ever had. We will be driving up tomorrow, if that is still okay?" Daniel asked.

"Yes, I was just going to call you. Everything is set up, and I will text you the address, etc. It's not a big fancy town around here, but the area is quite scenic and the air is pure. I agree it would have been more gumptious if Bella had called you or told you in person. A text is just a coward's way out. I'm glad that Aisha and you have forgiven her, and that you enjoyed your oysters. I remember you always saying that the world was your oyster. Today it is," Phoebe answered.

Phoebe told Isaiah what had transpired. "That little twat didn't have the nerve to call her brother, so she texted him."

"I get it, but don't let the little 'twat' piss you off. People her age hardly use the phone. They text about almost everything. I do agree that it was quite cowardly of her, but at least she listened partially to what you told her. If Daniel and Aisha can forgive her, I guess we can too," Isaiah tried to comfort Phoebe.

"Aargh! Bleh! You are right Isaiah, but it still pisses me off. Y*ou* are a better man than I am, Gunga Din. Thanks for listening. You helped me get it off my chest. I feel better now," Phoebe grumbled, and then smiled.

Daniel and Aisha got to their *Airbnb* late the next afternoon. They called Phoebe and told her that they were zonked from driving and would see them in the morning.

Dannie and Abby had left earlier in the day. They all had a fantastic time with one another, but both Phoebe and Isaiah were glad to have a short window of time where they could be alone with one another.

Daniel and Aisha stopped at a *Whole Foods* store in San Francisco. They stocked up on groceries that should last them for at least a week before heading north. Aisha liked the wooded roads and hills, as they got closer to their destination. It reminded her of home, but gentler, greener, and friendlier. The rental home was nice too, maybe not as fancy as Daniel's parents place, but more than adequate. They were tired after their drive, and checked in with Phoebe before going to bed to let her know that they had arrived.

Aisha and Daniel woke up real early, still being on an east coast time frame, and headed over to Phoebe's, after Aisha prepared an Afghan omelet. The omelet was different from an American omelet. First, Aisha diced up a potato with the skin still on, and fried them in the pan till they were crispy. Then she added cut up skinned tomatoes and a couple of sliced shallots, frying them until they caramelized. Then she poured four eggs that were not broken up, over the top of the potato mixture, with some green chilies, salt and pepper. They toasted some sourdough bread that they had bought in San Francisco. Eating this meal reminded them both of their former lives together in Afghanistan, though the bread and stove were better.

They were in a good mood when they got to Isaiah and Phoebe's cabin. Phoebe and Daniel both teared up when they held each other for the first time in years. It was quite touching. Aisha extended her hand to Isaiah, who took it in his hand in a friendly handshake.

"You look great Phoebes. You haven't aged a day," Daniel stated. He introduced his wife, who put out her hand, but Phoebe pulled her to her, and gave her a big hug instead.

"We are in America now, and we are practically family, so I think a loving hug is in order," Phoebe remarked.

"You are right. I am in America now. You are so very beautiful Phoebe," Aisha stated.

"Thank you, but you are seriously so gorgeous Aisha. I see why Bella got so jealous," Phoebe said, not having forgiven Bella totally.

Isaiah and Daniel also hugged each other. They seemed to like each other from first sight.

"I've seen you many times on television, Daniel. You were my second favorite reporter, after Phoebe of course," Isaiah light heartedly stated, as he was showing them the area around the cabin. All of a sudden there was a sound of rapid rifle fire coming from the area where the wolves liked to hang out. Then a lot of howling noises pierced the air.

"This is not good. It sounds like some hunters or poachers have fired on the wolves, or at least in that direction. I have to go and check it out right away. You can take our guests inside Phoebe. I'll get my rifle first," Isaiah said in a serious tone.

"I'll come with you. I have some experience with tracking and shooting from my days with the Taliban. Do you have an extra rifle, Isaiah?" Daniel asked, then he added, "Phoebe can you please stay with Aisha. As you can see she is quite along with her pregnancy and not fit for this kind of adventure."

"Will do, us women will stay back and watch the fort. Be careful and please call us frequently with updates. Okay?" Phoebe replied.

"Come on, we've got to hurry, Daniel. I've got a second rifle and a pistol, also locked up with mine that you can use. We don't want whoever shot that rifle to get too far away," Isaiah stated.

"I'm with you, brother," Daniel said, as they both ran toward where the wolves' den was, after getting their firearms.

They got there quickly and found Antonio whimpering and bleeding out some distance from the den itself. There was nothing they could do for him. He was one of the nicest wolves that Isaiah had known, very friendly and playful. Isaiah first took out his phone to chronicle the event.

"Please keep me out of any video or photographs. I'm trying to keep a low profile right now, you understand?" Daniel said.

"Of course, I just want to have a record of what happened here," Isaiah replied.

Isaiah then took out his pistol and shot the poor boy in the head to put him out of his misery. He asked Daniel to continue recording the event with his phone, because Phoebe might want it for her documentary, in addition it might be important for the police record. After finishing off the poor wolf, both Daniel and Isaiah noticed some footprints nearby. They had picked up the tracks of two large men wearing boots, or at least two people with large shoes. The hunters or rather killers were not difficult to follow, and our heroes found them in a gulley about a mile away.

"I'm going to call Mitch Godowsky, the Park Ranger assigned to this area," Isaiah whispered to Daniel, then whispering into the phone the exact location they were at, and why he was calling.

"I can be there in about 30 minutes Isaiah. I have your phone in my system and I can track it. Don't do anything foolish. Stay back, but follow them if you need to," Mitch said.

The two wolf killers were taking a break and eating some food, where Daniel and Isaiah could keep an eye on them without revealing themselves.

Ranger Mitch showed up as he promised in about 30 minutes. The two men were about to take off again, but Mitch along with Isaiah and Daniel stopped them in their tracks. Isaiah took out his phone to video record the scene.

"Hello there fellers. Do you know it's illegal to hunt in the state forest this time of year?" Mitch asked.

"Officer, we are not hunting. We are just hiking around the area."

"Then you wouldn't mind if I checked your rifles to make sure that they haven't been used recently," Ranger Mitch asked politely.

"Okay, we did a little target practice a little while ago, but we didn't hunt any animals," the taller of the two men lied.

"I'm afraid that a wolf has been shot less than a mile from here, less than an hour ago. We are going to retrieve the bullet from it, and if it matches the ones from your rifle, which I have the authority to take from you, then I would say, you will be found guilty. I'll need both of your driver's licenses please," Mitch calmly stated.

"Okay, okay. We shot the filthy critter. They are evil and dangerous. We were doing a service. How about we give each of you a couple hundred dollars to make this disappear," the hunter, who seemed to be in charge, offered.

Isaiah felt himself getting heated, and it took all of his self control from punching the despicable fellow.

"I'm afraid that I am going to have to arrest the two of you now. Trying to bribe a government official is a crime. Put your hands behind your back," Mitch said, as he cuffed them and read them their Miranda rights.

Isaiah felt somewhat vindicated from Mitch's tough response, and felt his anger dissipate to some extent. They all hiked back to the road, and Mitch put the two law breakers in the back of his ATV, along with putting their rifles in the trunk, and thanked both Isaiah and Daniel for their service.

"I'll get the bullet from Antonio's corpse before we bury him, and bring it to the station shortly," Isaiah stated, as he and Daniel walked back to the den.

Once in the car, the leader of the two villains said, "Okay, now that it is only you, and the wolf-loving coon is gone, we can offer you a substantial handout for letting us go free."

"Shut up. You don't want to get into any more trouble than you are already in," Mitch replied instantly, as he drove to the ranger station.

Chapter 22
Aisha Phoebe Daniel Isaiah and the Wolves

Voices were emanating from the video feed that Isaiah had set up. The two women moved to the TV screen so they could watch some of the feed from the wolf den. They saw Isaiah's back, shooting at one of the wolves lying on the ground. "He probably had to put that wolf out of its misery. That was painful to watch. I hope our guys will be okay," Phoebe said, as the video went silent.

"They are both very capable, and I think that they will be fine," Aisha responded, hoping to have both Phoebe and herself as well feel better.

The two women were getting to know one another. Phoebe made some coffee for Aisha and herself.

"That's a good attitude Aisha," Phoebe remarked. "Isaiah and Daniel are both very capable of taking care of business. Thank you for reminding me."

"This is really good coffee. You make it strong like we used to drink at home when we could get our hands on any. I have found most American coffee to be too weak, but I really love almost everything about this country. There is so much stuff. I can't believe your stores. They are filled wall to wall with stuff. Nice stuff, not so nice stuff, all kinds of stuff. The department stores in New York were overwhelming, all kinds of clothing stuff and linen stuff and furniture stuff. It's not like in Afghanistan, where we have hardly any stuff. Then the supermarkets, every aisle with all kinds of food stuff. There was a whole long aisle packed with all kinds of cereals. What kind of cereal do you like Phoebe?"

"You are funny Aisha, with your use of the word stuff, but right on, nonetheless. To answer your question, I never go to those cereal aisles. I like to shop along the outside aisles of supermarkets. That is where the most healthy products are. We like to eat fresh food most of the time. Isaiah knows some local ranchers, where we get eggs and cheese, seasonal vegetables and fruits, and some meat on occasion. He also bakes his own bread here. Do you like bread Aisha?"

"Do I like bread? The bread in Afghanistan was not so great, but I found the breads that Mrs. Granger had in her freezer to be so yummy. They were delicious fresh, but she put them in the freezer to keep better, if we did not eat them right away. She had delicious New York rye breads and pumpernickel. She would toast them if frozen, but when they were fresh I liked them without toasting, with some avocado or jam. I loved those sesame and poppy seed bagels she had too. We have a lot of poppies in Afghanistan, but no real bagels. Mrs. Granger served us bagels with smoked salmon one morning that was so delicious," Aisha responded enthusiastically.

"Isaiah also smokes his own salmon. I grew up eating bagels. I still crave them, but they are not as good here on the West coast as the ones in New York. It could be how they boil them, or that the New York water is perfect for bread. I once did a story on bagels. It seems that they were first created in Poland. They developed from the large German bread similar to pretzels, which German immigrants brought there. Jews were not allowed to be bakers, because of the Catholic prejudice against them due to how they view that the Jews were responsible for Jesus's crucifixion, even though it was really the Romans who punished him. A Polish Prince named Boleslaw in the thirteenth century wanted his country to be more secular, and ordained that Jews could be bakers. However a Catholic Bishop got in the way of Jews baking, saying they would poison the Catholics. Hence, Jews were only allowed to bake if they boiled the dough first, so bagels were invented."

Phoebe continued, "I heard another story about a baker in Austria a few centuries later, who wanted to celebrate Jan Sobieski, the Polish King who helped save Austria from the invading Ottomans. Sobieski loved horses, and the baker baked the bread to look like a horses' stirrup. The word for stirrup was beugel. Hence the name bagel was invented. These are just stories, and we have to take them with a grain of salt, which isn't bad on a bagel either," Phoebe related.

"I like those stories. I like history too," Aisha said.

When Isaiah and Daniel got back to the wolf den, the other members of the pack were all around their dead brother and uncle, sniffing and licking his body. Even Rebecca had left her litter inside and had come out to grieve. They were all howling in a low deep sound in a lament to their fallen comrade. They allowed Isaiah to remove the bullet and to bury Antonio in a grave, not too far from the den, still lamenting his loss.

Isaiah and Daniel had bonded over the tragedy. They walked back to the cabin in a somber mood, but at least feeling that they did what they could, and hopeful that justice would prevail.

"I think how unfair it is that humans have used their big brains for destruction instead of in loving ways. Wolves have a hard enough life without hunters coming along and shooting them, so just let them be. Help them out, don't harm them," Daniel said to his new friend.

"I guess you are singing to the choir here Daniel, so I agree with you 100%. At least we have three more little wolves almost ready to make their appearance, and the pack can fortunately afford the loss of one member. Last year we had those three yearlings born that you just met. They were all males. This year another three, and two are females, so the pack is still thriving," Isaiah informed his new buddy.

The two women greeted their men with open arms and relief that they were not harmed. "Did somebody shoot at one of the wolves, like you thought Isaiah? We saw you having to put one of them out of its misery via the camera feed," Phoebe asked. "Why didn't you call or text us? We were worried. Well, not too much, but you could have communicated with us."

"Yes, I'm sorry, you are right dear, we should have. I got carried away with the excitement. They shot Antonio. I had to put him out of his misery, which is so difficult. We followed the perpetrators, and called the ranger, who came in quick time. He arrested the perpetrators when they tried to bribe us. I've got to go back out to town now and give them the bullet that we just retrieved from Antonio. I think the pups will be coming out of the den soon, and I checked the cameras and they are all set. We also took footage of the dead wolf, and the two murderers, and their arrest. It will at least add some excitement to your documentary, and demonstrates some of the problems that wolves face."

"Apology accepted, I realize how much you care for your pack. The video footage is a good idea Isaiah. It will show the difficulty that wolves have in maintaining their population, plus add some unwanted yet exciting drama," Phoebe responded.

After Isaiah took off, Daniel was left with his two pregnant wives. "It seems that you two are getting along. I really like Isaiah too. He is a dedicated and an effectual young man. He handled the situation flawlessly."

"We are getting along. We had some tea, and Phoebe has been regaling me with stories about bagels and bread, and I have been telling her about all the stuff that I have encountered in America. I am glad that you weren't injured.

She was worrying about you and Isaiah. I told her that if you could survive in war torn Afghanistan that these forests are tame in comparison," Aisha replied.

"That is very true. I felt safe the whole time, and as I said, Isaiah can really handle himself too. It is nice up here Phoebe. Your cabin is a little funky from the outside, but in here it is quite comfortable and luxurious, especially compared to how we lived in Afghanistan. I love that painting over your bed. Where did you get that, and who is the painter?" Daniel asked.

"Actually the artist was just here yesterday, and gave it to us as a housewarming gift. She is a beautiful blond woman who lives by herself with her dog in Bolinas. We met her at the beach there on our first date and became instant friends. The two vortexes of energy are how she sees Isaiah and me relating," Phoebe answered.

"Oh that reminds me. We have a little gift for you too. It's a year supply of baby diapers that will be mailed monthly to wherever you want. They are biodegradable too, which I know you care about. I think that it is more than coincidental that you and Aisha will both be giving birth this year. I think that it would be so wonderful if we could all live close to one another at least," Daniel said.

"Well, Isaiah recently received a job offer to take over for his mentor in Missoula, Montana, which is not all that far from Colorado, where you said that you would be living," Phoebe stated.

"I think it's actually about 900 miles apart, which I wouldn't classify as being neighbors, but it's a start. These western states are huge, and the whole state of Wyoming is in the way. Maybe once the babies are born we could check out Missoula. I am serious about wanting to live closer to you. Aisha doesn't have any friends in this country, and she seems to have taken to you. I travel around anyhow, all over this country and the world, as you know, and with newborns I don't see Aisha coming with me on many of these trips. It would be nice if she had people that she liked and could trust, to be close by."

"I don't know many folks in Missoula either, so I am in favor of bringing good neighbors to the area such as you and Aisha. However, Isaiah still has not made up his mind if we are going there, but I think we will. It is a great opportunity, and he will be hired to give classes at the University too, as that is what his predecessor did. He probably will get some graduate students who will learn from him. He knows a lot about the wilderness, and how to assist the animals that live there. It will be more populated and civilized in Missoula than out here, but there is plenty of wilderness nearby. I even did a story a couple of years ago for a magazine on his mentor, the aforementioned Hootman that I traveled to Missoula for. It is a very nice town."

"Do you ever think about doing TV again? You were so talented, and loved by your audience?" Daniel asked.

"I think my days on the News are over, but I am working on a documentary now about the wolves around here," Phoebe answered. "How about you Aisha, do you have any ambition to be on TV?" Phoebe asked.

"I never thought about that. I think that I will first be a mother and a wife, and then maybe do something that I never have done before, like Television," Aisha responded.

"I think you would be great on TV. You are beautiful, young, and speak so well, and in more languages than just English. You could at least get a job with *Al Jazeera,* if not *ABC*. Don't you think she would be great, Daniel?" Phoebe questioned her ex.

"Aisha is very talented and brilliant. I hadn't thought about that either, just escaping recently, and everything being so new to her. She is picking things up really quickly though. I think that her being in front of the camera is an excellent idea. I think I will bring it up with Fred and Catherine over at corporate, and see if they can give her a job, once the twins are born that is, if you want to Aisha. I also know some people over at *Al Jazeera* who would probably jump on the idea. With Covid still around, it is quite normal to work from home these days and she can probably start as soon as she wants to too," Daniel stated, getting loving glances from his present and past wives.

Isaiah did not take long to return. "There is a possible two years of jail time plus a hefty fine, and Mitch thinks that we have enough proof to put those two characters away. They are still in holding, and probably will be released on bail today or tomorrow, but may have to plead guilty, as the evidence is overwhelming," Isaiah exclaimed, without stopping to catch his breath.

Phoebe came up to him and put her arms around him, and gave him a big squeeze to bring him back into his body.

"Thanks, I needed that," Isaiah said. "I am also leaning toward deciding to take the job in Missoula, if that is all right with you, Phoebe. I think that I can do more good teaching others and getting the word out than trying to save the wolves all by myself. Wolves are better protected here in California than in Montana, but after today we can see that even when protected they still are hunted. Plus, there will be a bit more civilization around to help with your soon to be delivery drawing near."

"We were just discussing that too. Aisha and Daniel want to check out Missoula as well, once their babies are born. We don't have to decide today," Phoebe stated.

"Maybe we can skip going to Colorado all together and go straight to Montana. I don't know anyone in Colorado anyhow. We can rent a place first and then see about buying a home there, if we like it," Aisha said, surprising her husband.

"Hmm, let me think about that. Okay, I thought about it. If that is what you would like, then we can do that. I do like the hospital in Colorado, so maybe we can live in Colorado for a short time and then move to Missoula. It does get cold there in the winter, I do have to warn you, though it is probably the most temperate area of the whole state. It is not that much different from Afghanistan, though winter usually lasts longer and starts earlier. At least there won't be any paparazzi there. We can probably get a second place in San Diego or even go to Mexico when it really gets cold," Daniel responded quickly.

"So you are going to just leave us alone in Missoula when a little freezing weather arrives?" Phoebe chided her ex, jokingly.

"You can come with us," Aisha said, assuaging the conversation, not realizing that Phoebe was kidding her ex.

"Oh yes, we can bring the wolves with us too, so they won't get frost bit," Isaiah teased.

"They are kidding us Aisha. This is American humor," Daniel stated.

"Ha Ha," Aisha rejoined.

At that moment of levity there was a beeping from the cameras set up by the den. The three pups were about to make their debut on the outdoor stage.

"We should get over there quickly," Isaiah said, "if we want to witness this rare show. Everything will be recorded anyhow, but it will be fun to share this with you all, being that you have never seen it before. You can wear these skull caps and dark glasses, Daniel and Aisha, so no one will recognize you, if you are caught in the recording."

They all hustled to the den, which was about a mile east of the cabin through the small path in the woods. As they arrived, Rebecca was leading her pups out of the den.

"That's Rebecca the mother, and alpha female, leading her pups from the den. The large dark male with his tail held high is Barack, the proud father. The pup that is almost pearl colored we named Cora Pearl. The other whitish female we named Lulu White, and the third male pup, the darkest one, we called Henry for King Henry," Phoebe explained, feeling like a proud grandmother.

"We named them on their day of birth, about three weeks ago," Isaiah confided.

"The three middle sized males hanging over there are Looey, Dewy and Huey, who were born a year ago. Isaiah named them, and thought about changing their names to more grownup ones this year, but I persuaded him to keep their original names, because it fits their personalities I think," Phoebe clarified.

"So last year was cartoon characters and this year it's prostitutes and a womanizer. I think that is creative," Daniel laughed.

"I've never seen a wolf in my life, except perhaps for Daniel. I'm kidding my love," Aisha joked, and then recanted, after seeing the frown on Daniel's face. "The little ones are so cute. There are supposed to be some wolves in Afghanistan, but if there are, none of my friends or family or myself have seen any for many years. The forests are rapidly disappearing there, as the timber industry is not regulated, and deforestation is a major concern, along with the disappearance of the larger mammals. However, there are a lot of feral dogs in Kabul. They roam the streets at night in packs, so it's kind of like wolves, but not. I don't know who Looey, Dewy and Huey were, but I think those names are perfect for those three," who had just come up to Aisha and licked her hand to say hello. "The puppies are so small too, with such blue eyes," Aisha reported.

"They will grow up fast now. They have already more than doubled in size since they were born less than three weeks ago. Their eyes won't stay so blue either, becoming more yellow gold like the older ones. You can see how much growth they have in just a year, if you compare their older brothers to them; by two years they are fully grown. Most of the growth occurs in their first year. I think Rebecca and Barack must have brought them out of the den a bit early, probably due to the excitement from their Uncle Antonio being shot. They all look healthy at least," Isaiah said, as he hugged Phoebe close to him.

This was a real emotional day for Isaiah, and hugging Phoebe had him feel more grounded, as well as for her. The pack seemed to be having ambivalent emotional feelings too. They were glad of the new members, but sad from the death of their old buddy, or maybe that was how Phoebe interpreted their moods, because that was how she would feel if she were them, and she didn't think they were that much different.

Later in the day toward evening, Daniel and Aisha were regaling Isaiah and Phoebe with stories of how they met and fell in love.

"I was already working on computers when Aisha joined the group in the kitchen. She, as all the women there, was wearing a burqa, so I could not see her face or her figure. However, she was sending strong signals to me, and was giving off sexy vibes despite that, through her clothing. I felt that way every time she served the meal, and was having dreams about what she looked like underneath. I could tell that she was young, fairly tall, and was far more beautiful than the others there, at least that is what I imagined."

"Daniel had a long beard when I met him. I knew he had been injured in a drone strike, and that his memories were very scattered. The other single women in the kitchen were all having fantasies about him. They thought he was so handsome and brilliant too. This intrigued me even before meeting him, as I was only supposed to be in the kitchen and not to do any serving of the men at first, as I was the youngest. Eventually one of the serving girls got sick and I had to take her place. I also thought that this man is indeed handsome and younger than I thought. I started flirting, or my perception of what flirting is, with Daniel surreptitiously, so the others would not interfere. He started noticing me, and I felt a bond or something growing between us."

Aisha continued, "I had never been with a man before, and this one intrigued me like no other had. I am not even sure what I did to get his attention, as we don't talk about flirting, and or sex, growing up in a strict Muslim household under Sharia law. Anyhow, he seemed to take an interest in me, and we started to meet late at night and talk. He was able to get me to come over to his communication work detail, and help him with computer work, which no other women were allowed to do. I picked it up fast, and we enjoyed each other's company. I guess I had a huge effect on Daniel because shortly thereafter he asked me to marry him, and he quickly got the approval of his higher ups to do so. My family was poor and did not live too far from our compound. My father was glad that I was to be married. Daniel promised to take care of them when he got some money, and they readily agreed to the wedding, which was small for Afghan standards, with only the folks from our compound, and a few members of my family attending. After we left this past year, he actually kept his word and sent them more money than they ever had before," Aisha related, and went on with her story.

"Daniel seemed to remember more and more languages, and taught me many of them. We both are polyglots, so I also picked them up quickly. He also remembered how to perform in the bedroom, probably never forgot that, and I was pleasantly surprised to how much fun one can have between the sheets."

"Talking about being pleasantly surprised," Daniel added and continued. "When I finally got to see Aisha undressed, and not wearing her burqa, albeit not in bright lights or sunlight, I was overwhelmed with her beauty and loveliness. She had perfect skin and her whole anatomy was perfectly in tune to my vision of what a beautiful woman can look like. Her face, as you can see, is gorgeous. I had hit the winning numbers of the marriage lottery. It was not difficult to perform my matrimonial duties with a beauty such as Aisha."

"I am so glad that things worked out for you. I was a total wreck for a long time, thinking that you were dead, Daniel. I have also hit the jackpot with Isaiah. I found two great husbands in my short life. Isaiah and I have not officially tied the knot, but we will before our baby is born," Phoebe responded.

"Did you know when you were doing it that you were creating a baby? I had a strong feeling when I became pregnant. The sex we had was far better than what we had previously. I got on top of Daniel after he had sucked on my pussy for a long time. I was feeling so tremendous and wanted to reciprocate those sensations to him. I rode him bareback like he was a wild stallion and I was a rodeo star. Isn't that what you call those cowboys or cowgirls?" Aisha asked, speaking intimately with her new friends.

"Thank you Aisha for feeling safe enough with us to talk like that. Most people, even our closest friends, are very guarded talking about their sexuality. I knew right after we had intercourse that I was pregnant, and told Isaiah my intuition. He did not really believe me, because good sex and getting pregnant don't have to go hand in hand, and yes, rodeo star is a good analogy." Phoebe replied.

"Oh thank you for saying that Phoebe, I didn't know about the etiquette, though I probably should have. I never spoke to anyone about sex before. It is also taboo in my old country to do that. It just felt natural to speak to you about it. I hope I did not embarrass myself, or you," Aisha rejoined.

"No dear, it is really fine. Perhaps the old me would have felt that way, but I have been opening up about sexuality lately. We actually had a little orgy recently with two other women and us. One of them was a new friend who was visiting us, and we had a threesome the night before with her. So I've been in a threesome and a foursome this week. I even kissed, and had my pussy licked by another woman. I hope I did not embarrass anyone," Phoebe stated, hoping to make Aisha feel her friendship, and starting to feel turned on from being able to express herself about what she had done.

"You men have been quiet since we started this intimate conversation," Aisha said, feeling some turn-on as well.

"I can feel your turn-on Phoebe, and yours as well Aisha. Maybe we can have a toned down foursome here now. I can kiss Phoebe and Daniel can kiss you Aisha to start, that is if you would like that?" Isaiah asked, getting a bit red in his face from both turn-on, and embarrassment.

Both Phoebe and Aisha nodded their heads in approval and pulled their men into their arms, or actually got the men to pull them into their arms. They simultaneously got both Daniel and Isaiah to kiss their necks first.

The music was playing softly in the background, and both Daniel and Isaiah were kiss dancing on their ladies necks, and their faces, including their ears, cheeks and lips. It wasn't exactly choreographed, however the rhythms were similar, and then the two women were kissing back on their guy's lips.

Chapter 23
Phoebe Isaiah Aisha Daniel and Company

"Well, I'm feeling that we all are in agreement here. I know it's okay with me. We can even do a little partner swapping, if it happens to go in that direction," Phoebe said quickly, and then went back to kissing Isaiah.

"I never had sex with anyone besides my husband, and it turns me on thinking of Isaiah sucking on my pussy and playing with his cock," Aisha seconded the notion.

"You must know that I'd love to make love to Phoebe again. I wouldn't want just anyone touching Aisha of course, but I feel good about my brother Isaiah and Aisha having some fun."

"I'm game to whatever," Isaiah responded, as he lavishly kissed Phoebe some more where she could feel his tongue on her lips and inside her mouth making her pussy tingle.

Everyone took off their clothes and got completely naked. "I got an idea. How about we all focus on Aisha and the three of us can give her a group groping?" Phoebe offered.

Aisha responded quickly. "I think it would be better if you went first Phoebe. Let us watch how Isaiah gets you off, and we will join in at an appropriate time."

"That is totally fine with me. Come on Isaiah," Phoebe rejoined, and the shenanigans began.

Isaiah sat by the left side of Phoebe, sitting perpendicular to her, his back against the headboard, and Daniel being left handed sat by her right side. Aisha started by sitting between Phoebe's legs so that she could watch the action.

Isaiah started playing with her left leg and told Daniel to follow his lead on her right leg. "You can play with her feet since you are sitting down there Aisha, if that is all right with everybody?" Isaiah asked.

"This is great. My two favorite men and the prettiest woman in the world are touching me. That feels so good Isaiah," as he was teasing her pussy now, as Daniel and Aisha both heartily agreed.

Phoebe started moaning as her orgasm intensified.

"That's amazing, you started having contractions, Phoebe, as soon as Isaiah barely touched your pubic hair with his palm," Aisha described.

"Now I am going to put some lubricant on these two fingers and lubricate her labia. She usually likes it on the left upper labia the most," Isaiah explained, as Phoebe reacted perfectly with even more intense contractions when he touched that area.

He repeated going up and down her labia, with Phoebe's orgasm increasing. He then dipped his finger just at the surface of her wet vagina, and stroked up and down her introitus. He got incrementally closer and closer with his upward strokes, finally touching the lowest part of her clitoral head. Isaiah then put a small glob of lubricant on his index finger, pulled back her hood with the thumb of his right hand and landed right on the upper left quadrant of Phoebe's now exposed clitoris. The sensation jolted higher, as Phoebe moaned louder.

"I can even feel those strokes on my pussy, and it feels really really good," Aisha remarked.

Isaiah was playing Phoebe's pussy like it was a musical instrument and he was hitting all the right notes. He stayed on her favorite upper left pocket for numerous short strokes that brought Phoebe higher and higher. Isaiah deliberately brought the intensity down a little by moving his hand slowly lower to the bottom of her clitoris, and even back on her introitus for a couple of longer strokes, before getting back to her special pocket, to build the intensity again. Phoebe was baying like a wolf in heat now.

"Okay, how about you, Daniel? Why don't you give Phoebe some peaks from your side?" Isaiah interjected.

"That would be awesome," Daniel said, as he immediately placed his left index finger on her exposed and fully engorged upper left quadrant, his left thumb anchoring the stroke on the right side of her clitoris so that his stroking finger did not slip off.

"Aiyee, your hand feels real nice on my spot, Daniel darling. Maybe a little less pressure please. Yes, that is perfect. You got it. You got me good now. Keep doing just that," Phoebe proclaimed, as her orgasm started to pick up again.

Daniel repeated the techniques he quickly picked up from Isaiah, to bring Phoebe up by using short strokes on her favorite upper left spot, and then bringing her down for a few seconds with longer strokes on her pussy, down to her perineum and back up again. The first time that he returned to the spot after bringing Phoebe down a little, it felt like a magnet was pulling his finger to the exact location, similar to a smart missile honing onto its target. When his finger touched her sacred spot, he could feel the energy travel up that finger, up his left arm, into his body, his heart, his head, and his penis. His ears felt hot.

Meanwhile, Phoebe's orgasm spiked to a new height. "I can feel that sensation down into my toes and up into my head, and then out of my body," Phoebe reported.

"Your orgasm is energizing the room. I can feel my pussy even more," Aisha exclaimed.

"This is so great Phoebe. It's fun to do you, and also watching you getting off, and you are so filling the room with your orgasmic energy. It's all over us, and even bouncing off the walls," Isaiah remarked.

Aisha went from sitting by Phoebe's feet, and carefully sat on her chest, bending her head over Phoebe's face. Her large belly was draping over Phoebe's torso. She began gently kissing Phoebe's lips with her own. Phoebe was moaning, and Aisha's lips were reverberating from the orgasm being released from Phoebe's throat through her mouth, and the two girls were having muffled moans back and forth, as Daniel continued to take Phoebe higher. The kissing action increased with more pressure being used, plus Aisha was now penetrating Phoebe's mouth with her tongue. Phoebe wrapped her own tongue against Aisha's. Isaiah lay down between Phoebe's legs, and began to suck and lick on her thighs, and all over her pussy, except her clitoris, which Daniel was attending to with much focus.

"I believe we must be in heaven," Daniel stated, as the only one left in the room, whose mouth was not occupied.

At that same seemingly heavenly moment, the door was thrown open. Three armed and masked men stood there with their guns pointed at the four lovers on the bed. Again, Daniel was the only one who immediately saw what just transpired. Phoebe, Isaiah, and Aisha heard the disturbance soon after, and the heavenly revelry immediately stopped.

"Look what we have here Joe," the man in the red flannel shirt said.

"I'd say this must be some kind of satanic worship," Joe, wearing a black jacket, responded. The third man in navy blue just grunted his agreement.

"I recognize you John Phillip Wheedle. You are the man who killed the wolf today," Daniel calmly stated. Being a polyglot, Daniel could recognize accents, and remember voices, like someone with perfect pitch, similar to a photographic memory, but of sound.

The man in the red flannel shirt pulled off his mask. "You are pretty clever my friend. I guess we are going to have to kill all of you now, not just the coon," John Phillip countered.

"You never said anything about killing anyone. You just said that you wanted to scare them. Besides, I recognize the white guy. He's the TV personality who just escaped from Afghanistan. That must be his pretty young Muslim wife. The other lovely lady looks familiar too," Joe responded.

"I don't care who they are. They know who I am, and that guy knows your voice by now as well. There is no other option," John Phillip loudly answered and continued. "Let's tie them up with these zip ties, and take them outside into the forest, and put them out of our misery. We can then bury them in the forest, where no one will ever find them."

"Okay, if you say so boss, but I don't like it. Should we have them dress first?" Joe asked.

"Why should we do that?" John responded, muttering, "You numbskull," under his breath.

Joe and the quiet third man tied up the 4 lovers, although reluctantly, as John Phillip held the gun on them.

"I know your heart isn't in this Joe. We forgive you," Daniel said, hoping to use psychology to change his mind perhaps.

"Shut up or I will kill you right here," John Phillip shouted.

The third man put a blanket and a sheet around the two women, as he was getting turned on by the sight, after tying them up.

"Okay, good, now everybody outside," John Phillip ordered. "You first," he pointed at Isaiah, using the N word.

They all filed out of the cabin. As soon as they were outside, loud howls were heard. Two wolves jumped out of the dark and took down two of the three would be murderers. The third man untied Isaiah to have him get the wolves off of his friends. The two men dropped their guns, as the wolves bit their arms.

Isaiah responded, leaping into the loud melee, and first getting Pippa off of the reluctant Joe, who just thought that they were coming along to support their bigoted friend, who wanted to scare and to terrify the wolf man. By the time Isaiah got to John Phillip, it was going to be too late. Barack had him by the neck, and blood was pouring out of his jugular vein. Isaiah finally got Barack to let him go, but by then he had lost too much blood and was unconscious. Phoebe gave John Phillip one last kick to get it out of her system.

Joe was still bleeding, but the injuries were not too bad, and he was alive. No major damage was perpetrated upon him.

Isaiah took charge of the situation, He had everyone go back into the cabin. He had the bleeding Joe sit at the kitchen table, applying a tourniquet to his arms, while Daniel, Phoebe, and Aisha got fully dressed. Aisha volunteered to wash the wounds with antiseptic soap that Isaiah handed to her, while he also got dressed. Isaiah got out his first-aid kit and began to sew up the injuries with sutures. He was an expert in treating minor injuries, having taken courses in first aid at school, plus occasionally having to do so out in the field. Isaiah finished the stitching up very quickly. Joe and the third man, who finally divulged his name as Orson, were very grateful and apologetic, saying how sorry they were for this whole incident.

"What do you think we should do with them?" Phoebe asked.

"I believe they were victims here too of their hateful friend, and deserve a second chance. However, I think we all have to agree on that. What do you all think?" Isaiah questioned his friends.

Both Aisha and Daniel were agreeable to letting them go, but Phoebe wasn't so sure.

"How do we know that they won't come back and try this again?" Phoebe asked.

Joe and Orson both pleaded with Phoebe, crying like babies. "We just came along because John Phillip asked us to. We would never have harmed you. Please forgive us. We will do whatever you want us to, but please don't turn us in. We have wives and children at home who rely on us."

"Well, I guess this is a time for forgiveness, so since the rest of my family have forgiven you, I will do so too. However, if you ever show up here again, your goose is cooked," Phoebe stated with authority.

"I am so sorry. This has been a nightmare for me too, and I can only imagine how you must feel," Joe stated, feeling that he had received a very kind pardon from these intended victims.

Orson said, "I will make sure that nothing happens to the wolves from the authorities for responding as they did. I know some influential people in town, so you won't have to worry about any blowback."

"Thanks, that might come in helpful. I will call Mitch again, and have him come and remove the body. We will stick to the story that John Philip acted alone, and that one of the wolves showed up in the nick of time, and saved our asses, and should be considered a hero," Isaiah declared.

"I think we should probably go out there and remove any footprints that these guys left, and check out if we have to clean up any blood splatter that the police might find. We don't want them finding more than Wheedle's blood out there," Isaiah remarked, still in charge.

"Good idea," Phoebe responded. "Orson and Joe can do that before leaving," she added.

"Yes mam, we certainly will do that. It's our own hides that we will be saving," Orson answered for himself and Joe.

The wolves had left as soon as Isaiah had taken back control and were nowhere to be seen. Isaiah set up some lighting for Joe and Orson to complete their job, and Daniel helped them clean the scene. Isaiah covered the body with a blanket, and then called Mitch, and described what had occurred, or at least the story they had concocted.

Joe and Orson left before Mitch showed up. Isaiah waited outside for Mitch. He arrived a few minutes after Orson and Joe had left.

"It's getting to be a habit Isaiah, you requiring my help. I guess John Phillip didn't learn from his first encounter with you and the wolves. This one ended even worse than the one earlier today," Mitch said, taking the blanket off of the dead body, trying to make light of a deadly serious situation. "I'll take your statement, and that of your friends, remove the body from here, and hopefully we won't have to bother you with any more legal obligations. I'll try to keep it low key, and let the district attorney know what happened, but they usually agree with my assessments. We do have to file all deaths, so we cannot sweep this totally under the rug."

"Great, thanks for helping out. If you need any more information, you know where to find me," Isaiah stated.

After taking down everyone's version of the incident, which was all pretty much the same, Mitch said. "I believe this wolf is the actual hero of the story. John Phillip could easily have killed the four of you, and we wouldn't have found out for days. I would say that this wolf was acting in self defense, even getting even for having his brother killed earlier, as well."

Isaiah helped Mitch put the bloody dead body into a body bag that Mitch had brought along, and they carried it into his vehicle. "So long Isaiah. As I said, hopefully you won't be hearing about this again."

"Take care Mitch. Thanks for all your help today," Isaiah remarked.

Phoebe gave Isaiah a big hug as he walked back into their cabin. "This has been a day and an evening that I will never forget. Man did it have its ups and downs. Today was a wild roller coaster ride. I guess all's well that ends well, but has it really ended?" Phoebe asked.

"I believe that the drama is over for the time being. We can let out a big exhale and appreciate that we are still alive and well," Isaiah responded.

"I think sometimes, maybe that it's me that all this psychodrama follows around," Daniel stated.

"Oh, I don't know about that. It seems we are all responsible for what shows up. Maybe you a little more than the average Joe, dear Daniel," Phoebe commented, as everyone laughed at her comment.

"I think that you and I Daniel should drive back to our place now, and leave these two amazing people alone to relax and come down. It was really fun having the sexual escapade that we were having before we were so rudely interrupted, I'd like to add," Aisha reflected.

"It's really been a pleasure and a half getting to know you Aisha. You are quite amazing yourself. We will have to continue our quartet party at some other time. I think that I am going to take Isaiah to bed now. We have to wash off this grime first though. Then the two of us will lie down and come down, as you said. I suggest that you two do the same when you get back to your place,"Phoebe declared.

"Thanks again for a wild and exciting day. I haven't felt this way since New York, and Germany, and Afghanistan," Daniel joked, hugging both Phoebe and Isaiah with a full embrace.

"Well, Isaiah, I'll wash your back if you wash mine," Phoebe said, as they walked back into their cabin after seeing Aisha and Daniel safely to their car.

"That sounds perfect to me. I'll even let you wash my hair, as I think I got a bunch of blood on it too. Luckily we weren't wearing any clothes when all that blood started gushing out there," Isaiah responded to his mate.

After cleaning up, both Isaiah and Phoebe were too tired to do anything but go to bed.

"This has been a very long day. We had a lot of fun between the crazy drama. I like both Aisha and Daniel. They are good people. I think when we move to Montana it would be nice to have them as close neighbors. I also will either have to train someone here to take over for me, watching over Barack and the pack, or take the pack with us, which is what I would prefer, if it is possible. They have become family to me, and today they proved their loyalty more than anyone could have imagined. You are a real trooper and buddy Phoebe, and I love you more than words can say. I can go anywhere now, and with you being there next to me, any place will feel like home. I am looking forward to our new adventure together," Isaiah whispered in her ear, as he held her tight under the covers, and proceeded to kiss her on her pillowy lips.

Acknowledgements

The characters in this book wrote this story. I may have created them to begin with, but they took off on their own directions, and searched each other out to develop their friendships. They also must have read one or more of my books about *Extended Massive Orgasm* to have become so proficient in giving and receiving sensual pleasure.

I would like to thank Jim and Jamie Dutcher for the inspiration that I got from reading their beautiful and true story, T*he Wisdom of Wolves*: *Lessons from the Sawtooth Pack,* published by *National Geographic* in 2018. Their tale of actually living with the wolves and video recording their daily endeavors into documentary films, provided much of the material for how Isaiah took care of his pack.

I also got a kick, and enjoyed the humorous book, *Don't Cry Wolf:* by Farley Mowat, published first in 1963 by McClelland and Stewart. It is written as a true story, though some of it was surely made up. Like Mowat says, he didn't want the facts to get in the way of the truth. His work helped pioneer much of the legislation aimed at saving the gray wolf from extinction. I also appreciate the work that Adolph Murie did to help protect the wolves from being wiped out entirely.

I'm thankful to Jack London, whose books I read when I was in my teens that probably helped inspire this story with his two books, *White Fang*, and of course, *Call of the Wild*.

I am grateful to Rudyard Kipling for writing *The Jungle Book,* and also for his *Gunga Din* poem, which both are mentioned in this book.

This book like all my others would never have been written, except for the love and feedback from my darling wife Vera, who is totally supportive of whatever I do.

I am appreciative to the nurses, aids, volunteers, and music therapists of *Home Hospice of the East Bay, plus Rey from Abundant Home Care* that have been helping me take care of Vera for the past months.

I'm very thankful to my friends, Bruce, Metzger, Pam, Vicki P, Vicki B, Diane, Frank, Trisha, Dave, our sons Tim and Tre and daughters Helen and Catia, and my twin brother Ron, for participating in my life situation, either in person, or on the telephone, while I was writing this story.

I am appreciative to all of you who have gotten to the end of this book and are reading my acknowledgments. I can be reached at stevebodansky@gmail.com or you can check out our website, extendedmassiveorgasm.com

Made in the USA
Monee, IL
14 March 2024

55051069R00115